1

The Second Shoot

Headlights shown brightly down the dark alley into John's eyes. Meagan held to the arm of his suit coat with a worried look on her face.

"What will we do, John?" She asked.

The motor shut off and all four doors of the sedan opened. Four men got out brandishing Tommy guns.

The one on the passenger side, obscured by the headlights, spoke in a familiar voice.

"There's nowhere left to run now. Give us the Talon."

John's eyes darted anxiously around. Finding what he was looking for, he grabbed Meagan by the wrist, and commanded her to follow. They darted down a crack between two buildings, shimmying to fit. They had narrowly escaped the hail of gunfire that had begun when John made his move. Now the aggressors gave chase. The leader who had spoke got back in the car with a driver.

"After them!" was his order to the other two. They obeyed, and shot through the same crack.

John and Meagan, on the next alley over, were running as fast as they could.

"Go that way!" John commanded, indicating an open back door. Meagan ran through, into a restaurant kitchen. Her red evening gown, and her sudden hurried invasion, caused a ruckus among the staff. She pushed through the throng of workers, and out the swinging door, into the dining room. Now she could try to blend in and hide. She righted her blonde hair as she made her way toward the bar.

Meanwhile, John had drawn his specially designed .32, and returned fire with the men on foot as he made his way up a ladder to the roof. The men followed. John dashed across the roof, and leapt the gap that they had shimmied through, onto the next building. The two men were in hot pursuit and made the gap as well. John kicked with all his might, trying to find some more speed. It would require all his athletic prowess for the next hurdle. Without any regard for thoughts of whether he could make it or not, John hurled himself over the alley below and onto the next roof. He rolled as he landed on the rooftop, coming to a stop against a doorway.

One pursuer lost his nerve, stopping short of the leap. Only just. Swinging his arms wildly for balance to not fall over the edge. The next man, who had been a step or two behind since the ladder climb, would not be so easily deterred. With a guttural sound, he heaved himself over the gap. John was up to receive him, as the man careened into him. They both fell back, crashing through the door and down some steps, into the attic of the building.

Now it was a fight to the death. John's pistol lay somewhere in the room, however the place was cluttered with all manner of items. There was no time to look for it. With both men now back on their feet, combat ensued. The thug came with a screaming, charging, right hand. John used his judo throw to send him over the top of him and into a table. Things fell all around. The man came up fast, his hand finding a heavy candle stick.

John looked frantically around as his opponent readied for another charge. A wooden rolling pin looked like as good a weapon as any. John brandished it like a saber. The candle stick came fast with an overhand strike. John presented the rolling pin to block. Now, with the weapons locked high, and his opponent's midsection open, John kicked, again sending the man into the table. This time the table gave way entirely.

Not willing to give up, the man made a bull rush at John, driving him back and through another door, despite John's repeated strikes with the rolling pin. There were more stairs beyond the door, and both men tumbled and struggled, as they went down them.

This time they fell into a carpeted hallway. A glance around told John that he was on an upper terrace of a dining hall. People at tables made exclamations of shock and fear at the men, as they continued to battle.

John's aggressor was a skilled and willing combatant. Despite John's many strikes, his defenses had been breached, and the man held John by the neck with both strong hands, and leaned him over a railing, threatening to send John crashing to the floor below, if he weren't strangled first.

Suddenly, with a shatter, John could breath again. The man's eyes went up and he melted to the ground. As the man went down, his absence revealed the blonde hair and pretty face of Meagan. In her hand she held the neck of a champagne bottle. She addressed John coyly.

"Need a hand, partner?"

John gave a wry smile and took Meagan's hand to help him off the railing. Now he led her down the staircase runner and toward the grand entryway. There they stopped short in their tracks.

"That's far enough." Menaced the voice from before. The leader stood before them in the entryway, flanked by his remaining two men, and their weapons.

John wasn't scared. He motioned Meagan behind his hip, and addressed the villain.

"We're walking out of here, Walters. You and your men need to step aside, if you know what's good for you. You'll never get the Talon."

The middle man laughed.

"You are outgunned, John. There's nowhere left to run. You must give me the Talon, or else."

Knowing he'd been beat, and that there was indeed no recourse. John's hand dove in his pocket, and pulled from it the Golden Talon. He tossed it on the floor, a few feet short of the leader's feet.

"There you go. Take it, and let us be." John spat.

The three men stepped forward. The head man bent down and lifted the Talon from the floor. He inspected it closely. He opened his mouth to speak, but John had something to say.

"Do it now!" He yelled.

Meagan sprung into action, taking John's gun from under the back of his coat. She rolled to one side, bringing the weapon toward the ceiling from one knee. Her target was a suspending chain for a large chandelier. Her shot rang out through the dining room. The light came falling down. It landed with a mighty crash, directly on the heads of the three men.

The room was now silent as the patrons looked on in shock. Meagan casually handed John his weapon back, and strolled toward the wreckage. The head man's arm protruded the perimeter of the heap, and in the hand was the Talon, shining and shimmering.

Meagan removed it from the dead man, and beckoned John to follow.

On the sidewalk outside of the restaurant, John grabbed her by the arm, turned her, and kissed her long. Now parted he spoke.

"You know you're going to have to let me have that, doll."

She looked down at the prize.

"I guess I will. It's a shame we can't just run away and hide with it.

John sighed.

"You know I've got a job to do for my country."

She placed the Talon in John's hand, and closed his fingers around it.

"Yes. I know you do, agent John Johnson."

"What the hell was that, Bob?" I asked, as the credits started to roll.

Bob, the usher at the theater, answered through a yawn.

"The Golden Talon, Mr. Trait."

"I know what it's called, Bob. I mean, when did he find his gun? How come the bad guys didn't shoot them when they first had them caught in the alley? Hell, the idea that a little .32 caliber bullet is going to shoot through a chain that's meant to hold up a thousand pound chandelier is ridiculous. And they call him a detective, but I don't remember a single piece of evidence being found or discussed in that entire picture."

Bob was getting himself out of a chair on the aisle, and responded to my criticisms.

"Well, I liked it alright."

I went ahead and let it go. It needs to be said, that Bob, while as nice an old man as you'll ever meet; I think has worked as an usher too long, and seen too many terrible pictures, to have any kind of good taste, at this point.

I took my feet off of the seat in front of me. I know it's bad manners, but aside from Bob and I, I wasn't sure if the projector operator had even hung around to watch that one. The place was deserted. I lingered in my seat for a bit longer to listen to the song that was playing over the credits. Throughout the film they had used pieces of it, and I rated that to be the only redeeming feature of the feature. Also, the lights hadn't gone up yet, so the whole thing was missing that feeling of finality. The one you get, after a good movie, when the lights come up and remind you that you don't live in a fantasy world, and for better or worse, The War didn't get won by a guy with his underwear on outside his pants, and the pretty damsel doesn't always want a kiss after a foot chase. It was the last show of the night though, so I decided I had logged enough complaints to Bob, and headed for the lobby.

The lobby was as deserted as the screening room had been. The concessions were all shut down, and the ticket booth was empty too. I even had to get into the coat room for my own jacket. There were a lot of unclaimed coats in there, by the way. I was surprised anybody might forget their overcoat during this time of year. It was January, and in downtown Chicago the wind was blowing and the air was freezing.

I took a moment in the lobby and counted my coins. I set up a number in my head, and the game was, if I had that much, I'd go ahead and take a cab home, but if not, then I would be realistic about how hard the times were for me, and brave the cold walk. The accounting did not yield satisfactory results. It was just a couple of days into the new year, and the gross income of the David and Trait Detective Agency had been goose eggs. I had had to get away though. By Friday we would have a little bit of cash to look forward to. My partner, David DeGrabber, was back at the office, with our two desks pushed right together, working his way through the third typed copy of an importer's ledger. Dave has a great head for that kind of work, but it makes me feel like leaping off a high dive into a puddle. I had to get away, so I took in the only movie playing at this hour. I checked my watch as I stepped out onto the cold sidewalk.

2

I don't know what time my watch said then. I got distracted. On the whole, I can be an appropriately single minded individual, but there are some things that I readily allow to break in on any regularly scheduled programming. Chief among them are gunshots. No sooner had I got the door opened, I was aware of a bright light shining in my direction. I thought it might be a parked car, but didn't take long to think it over. I had no more time before the sound of a shot hit my ears, and I hit the deck.

I'm a few years removed from my time in the Army, where I spent more than my allotted time in France, but the reflex to get down fast is still as sharp as ever. It's a useful thing to detectives anyway. You never know when somebody might take something very personally. Thoughts come fast in those moments too, as you go down and try to find a bit of cover to crawl to. One such thought that flashed across my mind, was the fact that I hadn't had my nose in anybody's business for nearly two months, so this must have really been an old grudge.

"Cut! Cut! Cut! Who the hell is that guy?"

That was a strange kind of thing for someone to yell in the midst of trying to gun somebody down. I had scrambled a couple of feet to a brick planter when another shot range out. The voice came again.

"Dammit, I said cut!"

That was followed by a clamoring of other voices and footsteps in the street. I held my hat up over the planter, and announced that I was coming out.

As I got to my feet the bright light blinded me. I held my hand over it to try to make out the scene. Someone said to cut the light off, and it was. I blinked as my eyes adjusted.

"What's going on?" I asked.

A man in thin rimmed glasses, a thin scarf, and not enough jacket, approached.

"Can't you see we're shooting a movie?" He pointed off to my right. There, at the corner of the theater, at the mouth of an alley, a man in a sharp hat and good overcoat, stood smoking. Around him was another man, with a kind of satchel around his waist, with a big pocket on the front. Beyond him, laid out on the sidewalk, was another actor.

The smoking man gestured impatiently my way.

"Come on, Fishman. Union cutoff time's coming." He held the cigarette in his mouth, and tapped where his watch would be on his coat sleeve.

The man with the thin glasses, Fishman, fired back.

"We're not in Hollywood, Stan. Just cool your boots."

"That's what I'm saying. My boots are freezing." With that he waved a dismissive hand our way and started into the street toward a group of people.

Fishman spoke to me.

"I'm sorry we startled you, sir. Walter Fishman, Director." He gave me his hand, and I shook it. "The theater told us there were only one or two people in there, and we thought we could get the scene finished before the last show let out. The cold has given us some technical difficulties."

"It's alright. It could always have been real bullets, meant for me. I'll take false alarms from here on out, if I can."

I was going to let Fishman have a little chuckle, a pat on the shoulder, and then be on my way, but instead we both froze. A terrible scream, from a woman, rang down the empty block. We turned toward the sound. At the mouth of the alley the fallen actor was still down. A girl in a heavy fur bent over him. She was giving it the works, with feet stomping, screaming, and hand gestures of all types. Fishman and I rushed over to see. A few others had beat us to it and all crowded around. Some murmured and some shouted. Their general message was that he was dead.

I pressed through the throng.

"Who's dead? Move out of the way. I'm a professional."

Some guy tried to shove me as I made my way in. I pushed him back and gave him a look that intimated he shouldn't try it again. He showed me his hands and stepped off.

It didn't take a pro to see what had happened. He had been a near middle aged man, but looked much younger than that. He had on black slacks, a big black over coat, shiny shoes, and crisp new hat, that sat a few inches from his head on the sidewalk. He had on a tie too; Red, over a white shirt. Now he had a badge of red under where the tie lay misplaced, right over his heart. I checked for a pulse as a formality, and said to no one in particular, that they needed to call the police.

A few people rushed off, hopefully to find a phone. I tried to take in the details. Whenever there's a fresh corpse made, the police want to know about it from everyone. What kind of pro would I be, if all I had was some, 'It all happened so fast, officer."?

There at the body, there wasn't anything to it. He was just laid down on the sidewalk, with his arms out to his sides, and one leg crossed under the other. It would have been as good a position as any if he had been acting it, rather than being totally committed to the role. In his right hand he held a .38 revolver, not unlike the one that I carried. Without disturbing the positioning, I got my nose to it, to see if I could detect whether it had been fired. It was tough to say. The smell of some trash cans was wafting down the alley, and the breeze was steady. I gave up on that, and told the remaining bystanders not to touch anything, or they could count on a night in the clink.

Next, I turned my attention to the obvious shooter. The other actor, Stan. I asked where he'd gone, and someone pointed to a little trailer, parked on the far side of the street. I started over toward it. As I approached the trailer door, I was intercepted by a young man that looked cold.

"Hey, you can't go in there."

I looked him up and down, and told him he should buy a better coat. I pushed passed him, and he grabbed me with both hands by my coat tail. I turned to him, real serious.

"Listen kid, I've seen a man or two get shot. Now, you may have a cold blooded killer in there, in the process of disposing of a murder weapon. Do you want to help him with that? Cause if you do, the law's gonna want some of your time too."

He let go, but continued his protest. At least now more civilized.

"Mr. Turner, doesn't have the gun. At the end of every scene, Mr. Law, our props man, takes the guns and reloads the blanks."

Now that was more like helpful.

"Where's this props man now? If you're telling it straight, then this Mr. Law mixed up a blank with the genuine article."

He motioned to follow, so I did. We walked a couple of parking spaces down to another trailer. My guide knocked on the back door. After a second of waiting, I pulled the door open, and looked in.

The inside was a wild scene. On the right there was a bench, and a rack above, with all kinds of projects in various stages of completion. On the other wall was a collection of swords, rifles, sticks, umbrellas, and any other item you could think of. On a rolling stool, halfway down the aisle, at a little clearing on the bench, sat the man I had seen with the satchel on his waist. He had the satchel inside out on the counter, and was inspecting a couple of .38 shells with a magnifying monocle. He looked startled at us, as the door opened and I came in.

"Put all of that down. Right now." I commanded, as I approached.

He talked fast in a high young tenor's voice.

"I'm trying to figure out what happened? All I have here are fired blanks."

I snatched the brass from between his fingers, and saw where the crimping had been. I shook him by the shoulder, nearly knocking him off the stool.

"Where's the live one, Law?"

His voice went up a little higher.

"I don't have any live ones. Do you know how dangerous that would be?"

"I just saw how dangerous it could be. We all did. Get up and get out of here. The police are gonna want to take a close look at all this. Go!"

He slid by me and joined the other kid outside. Another .38, similar to the one in the other guy's hand, was there on the bench. I took out a handkerchief and lifted the weapon by the barrel, so's not to smudge any prints from the more often handled parts, and gave it the sniff test. Sure enough, it had been fired. I had only seen one hole in the other guy, so the shooter had either missed, or there had only been one live round in it. Now I heard sirens outside. I sat the gun back where I'd found it and stepped out.

3

When I finally made it back to my little apartment, at nearly daylight, it and my bed looked like the best place in the world. This morning however, my mood was poor. The alarm clock that my mom and dad had sent me for Christmas sounded its two little bells on top at least two hours before I was prepared to hear them. It was the right time, after all; 7:30 sharp. I fumbled for the switch to shut it off, sat up, and took a little inventory of my whole life as I saw it.

There was my one linoleum floored room, that was going to try to freeze my feet off as soon as they hit it. In the same space, my kitchenette and fridge that was badly in need of a restock. Beyond, with more cold floor in store for me, was the bathroom and stand up shower, where the hot water might not last long enough for me to become a person again. It was a grim scene.

The radiator by the window was a bright spot. I got out of bed and made one cold footed stride toward it, and positioned my backside precariously close to the fins. The floor was warm all around it.

Now upright, the view of my little apartment was much better. I thought I'd get a rug for the middle the next time a had a few extra bucks.

I estimate it at only moments before my backside might have combusted, that I hurried to the shower. With that out of the way, and feeling a fair facsimile of myself, I dressed for my mile and a half walk to the office, down the January, Windy City, sidewalk. I picked out a black wool jacket, to go on under my overcoat, and some sharp leather gloves. Breakfast would be my last apple, en route. I hit the street.

I admit, my mood took another slight downturn during the walk to the office. The wind was worse than it had been the night before, and I had gotten plenty then. I made it though.

"Gosh, John, I can't believe you walked today."

It was Sid, our door man, at the four story building that held our office, and other units. He had a cup of coffee in one hand, and a smoke in the other. He looked kind of silly with his big brown overcoat draped over the shoulders of his service uniform.

"No money, Sid. Maybe you can start a car pool?"

He laughed his big goofy laugh.

"You know I take the bus."

I went on by and to the elevator. Getting off at the third floor, it was just a short walk down the hall to the frosted glass door and window. 'David and

Trait Detective Agency', was written on the glass in bold black lettering. Dave's first name, and my last. Dave's idea, apparently to instill maximum confusion in our callers. I gave a quick courtesy knock, and entered.

The whole scene was just like I had left it the night before to go to the movie. One big room, file cabinet at the back, some client's chairs along the left wall, and David DeGrabber, at his desk on the left, straight across as you enter.

He sat low and back in his chair, looking bored through his dark shaggy hair, and pecking at his typewriter. He had on his dark blue blazer, that he wore everyday. He'd been hard at it for the last week, and though he still maintained a slight heft to his frame, looked gaunt in the face, as if he hadn't remembered to eat anything. I tossed my overcoat and hat into one of the side chairs, and took my seat at my desk, directly across, facing Dave. I didn't see his eyes move any, but he spoke.

"John, you look absolutely haggard. I thought you went to a movie. Did you decide on drinks and dancing instead?"

"Move your feet out of the way." We were doing so much clerical work at the minute, that we had our desks pushed right together in the middle of the room, so we could save ourselves some steps. His long legs had been right under my chair. He pulled them in, and I continued.

"No dancing. Some kind of party though. It's gonna sound like a lulu, when I tell you. I was walking out of the picture, which was not worth the two bits, by the way, and a company was shooting another picture out on the street."

"That's unusual."

"Let me get to the unusual part. I didn't know what was going on. I walk out. I hear a shot. I hit the deck. Director starts yelling cut, cause I've messed up their scene, and another shot. Turns out, somebody put a hot one in the prop gun, and the guy acting shot, is shot."

In addition to having, what I assume to be, an everlasting reservoir of patience for typing ledgers, Dave contrastingly, has little capacity for getting excited. It must have been a real lulu indeed.

"Who was shot?" He sat up in his chair.

"Steve Roker. Stanley Turner pulled the trigger. Nobody even realized anything was wrong for a moment, till someone told the Roker guy he could get up."

"I take it you were delayed by the public's investigation."

"I was indeed. Detective Scott came down from the station with every one he had. They took a young guy that handles the props and the guns too, named Law, and arrested him."

"They determined him to be in charge of the conspiracy?"

"I don't know if it was quite all that, but they decided that he was the one that had loaded the gun, and so he must have wanted to pop this Roker."

"What sort of gun was it?"

".38 revolver, like mine."

"So, after realizing something was amiss, Stanley Turner checked and found a casing from a live round in the weapon?"

I held up a finger.

"Now that is a sticking point. The way I got it, after every scene, the guns used, get handed back to the props man for reloading, or safekeeping. It looked to me like Turner fired the shots, handed the gun back to Law, like always, and had a smoke. Turner claims to be totally ignorant about weapons. The police had most of us standing around freezing, when Turner busted out of his trailer, with Detective Scott on his heels. He was making a big show about how he was outraged that someone would dare accuse him of having knowingly harmed his fellow man. It's a strange position to hang to, if you ask me. The other actors said he's always playing a cop, or a goon, in most of his pictures, but doesn't ever do any reloading. Just pointing and shooting."

Dave had his arms crossed and his head down, absorbing the details. Now he looked up with a confused expression.

"I thought they only made films in California."

"I was under the same impression. I asked the director about that. His name is Walter Fishman. Clearly a Californian. By the way, none of that crew have enough jacket for the weather here. Anyway, his whole thing is that he takes this smaller group of actors around, and they shoot on location. He says, even though they've got a little Chicago street, or a fifth avenue, or a Mardi Gras parade, on a lot in Los Angeles, that you just can't recreate the grit and grime, he called it, of the real thing. I feel like a street's a street, personally."

"So what will happen now? A replacement actor and props person?"

"That's another wrinkle that I gathered while I was bopping around, trying to stay warm. The acting people-"

"Troupe."

"The what?"

"An acting troupe. It's a group of actors, or other performers."

"Oh. Well, the troupe says, 'the show must go on', and so does the director, but the city of Chicago, they say, has been trying to run them out of town since they got here last month. The council thinks it's disruptive to commerce, and they accuse the troupe of getting wild in their hotels and in the downtown spots."

I intended to go on, or at least start on a page of the ledger job, when Sid buzzed up from his desk downstairs. I got the switch and told him to go ahead.

"A, Mr. Fishman, to see you."

I told him to send him up. Dave had his hands behind his head and his feet under my chair, again, looking thoughtful.

A moment later, a familiar figure appeared in the hallway. He knocked and I got up to let him in. Fishman had on the same scarf and glasses as he had the night before, but this time had on an oversized French beret. It made him look artfully cold. We shook hands, and I directed the director toward the end of our desks. I got a chair from the wall and sat him down in it. He looked like he had been in some way misused since the last time I had seen him. I announced names, for introductions, and Walter Fishman shook Dave's hand nervously. Dave broke the ice in his professional way.

"Mr. Fishman, my colleague, Mr. Trait, has just been telling me of your misfortunes last night. It is a terrible accident."

Fishman was downtrodden and his voice was just a bit more than a murmur.

"It has been a terrible misfortune indeed, Mr. De-Grabber. These kind of accidents are unavoidable in our industry, but usually they happen under much more reasonable circumstances, and never to a member of the primary cast."

"What circumstances, yielding a workplace death, could be considered reasonable, Mr. Fishman?"

The director shrugged, and answered.

"It usually happens to a stunt man. He may be diving out of the way of a train engine, or jumping from a moving vehicle to another. Maybe he forgets, and steps on some explosive under the ground, and is injured, or worse."

I put in.

"In the Army we called that a land mine, Mr. Fishman. Nothing reasonable about that."

"How else can we make it to look as though shells are falling around a soldier on film? It's safer to blow a bit of earth up, with a small charge, than to launch something over head."

He had a point. I shrugged my shoulders, and let it go.

Dave moved on to business.

"Mr. Fishman, I doubt very much that you came today to lament the toil of the daredevil. What is it that brings you here?"

Fishman gathered himself and sat up straight. He might have made a noble figure, if not for the dainty hat and glasses.

"Your city means to stop the production of my

work. Now that this thing has happened, they intend to pull our permits."

"You explained, of course, that you believe it to be an unhappy accident?"

"I did, however there is the matter of the casing."

I narrowed my eyes at our guest.

"What's the matter with the casing, Mr. Fishman?"

"We can't find it. It's gone. Not only is it gone, but Rob, Rob Law, our props man, swears that it was never there."

Fishman was starting to get worked up, but Dave was calm, like always.

"I assume they have charged Mr. Law with murder, despite his testimony?"

"They have, but they also intend to charge Stanley Turner as an accomplice. Mr. Trait here, said that he was a professional detective, so since he had witnessed it all, I thought you would be my best chance."

"If the police have charged the two of them, for conspiring to kill one of your own, and are confident in their evidence, then I'm not sure there's anything for us to do."

The director shook his head.

"No. I refuse to believe that either of them would do something like this. We are a close knit group. This is the third project we have filmed this last year, with hardly any breaks for home. We are a family. Month before last, we were in New Orleans together, and Miami before that. Also, Stanley wouldn't jeopardize his chance. This was his first time to be the leading man in one of my films. Ally and Steve had helmed all the others. Stanley had to be good in this, because with the way he smokes, he might not look young enough to lead for much longer."

Fishman was starting to look bad. It wasn't much reasoning on his part. What he needed right now was lawyers, I thought. Maybe he had them working already. Dave seemed to think he could find some meat on the bone, and took a snap at it.

"Mr. Fishman, if we are to sort this out for you, and hopefully help you keep your leading man, we will need to talk to everyone in your troupe. It will be tiresome, but it is necessary. In the meantime, you may speak to Detective Bernard Scott, with the Chicago Police. Tell him you have hired us. We are friends of his. Possibly that might ease the pressure on the cancellation of your production. Is Stanley Turner out on bail?"

"Yes. I paid his bond this morning."

"Good. Send him to us as soon as you can."

Fishman held a finger aloft to point to a problem.

"Stanley won't come to you, I'm afraid. He's a unique individual. When working, he only sees outsiders in his private trailer. The film can survive without Roker, even if the rest of us struggle to, but we have to be able to use Stanley."

I could tell that had gotten under Dave's skin. He tapped a pencil on his pad impatiently. After a moment he closed his notebook and turned back toward his typewriter, and began the next entry into the importer's ledger. Without stopping he made some requests.

"Mr. Fishman, I would like all of Stanley Turner's films, and the means to view them, delivered to my home. John will provide you the address."

Fishman was taken aback.

"Now?"

"Yes, as soon as possible. The end of the day would be acceptable. You have access to them?"

"Well, I can have them sent by express, but I only have my own screen and projector, in my director's trailer-"

Dave was getting short with our guest now.

"I will procure one locally and bill it to you, or your company. Get his information, John."

I grinned and took it down. Fishman was over a barrel. I didn't much blame Dave for getting upset. Dave isn't the most delicate person I know, by a long way, and murder investigations are hard enough without the guy that you hope didn't do it, making it hard for you to help him.

I walked Fishman to the door and tried to tell him politely, to go find himself an overcoat. He said something about them not going with anything, so I just told him goodbye, and thought about how it was his funeral. I reclaimed my seat across from Dave. Dave didn't seem like it, typing and spacing from box to box on the ledger job, but I could tell he had picked up the pace a bit to get it over with so we could start on our new job in the movies.

4

Dave and I talked for a little while about what we should work on first. He volunteered to press on with the remainder of the ledger typing, and I said I would go and see what the officials knew so far. I say he volunteered, and he did, but I was attempting to influence his decision with my strongest telepathy. Those big typing jobs aren't so hard on the hands or back as regular detective work, but I find them far more taxing on the mind. And for what? You get another pile of pages to be filed away somewhere, should the tax man, or a customer armed with a litigator, come to highlight a discrepancy. The worst part would be, if it was the tax man, they probably wouldn't care what your paper pile said, and if it were an individual who bothered to hire a lawyer, then they were probably right anyway. We needed the money just the same. Dave held a position that we should start taking domestic cases, like the other agencies in town do, but I like to at least maintain the pretense of scruples, and held out that all we would do playing in that mud is get dirty. On the other hand, the alternative was typing things that no one cared about, so I found myself conflicted.

That was the sort of thing I let knock around in my head at the stop lights on the way downtown to the police headquarters, where our friend Ben Scott kept shop. Between the two of us, Dave and I, we are not entirely pedestrian. I borrowed Dave's blue sedan. It ran well enough, as long as I stayed on top of all maintenance. The sort of mechanical genius required to keep the oil and water topped off, was just beyond Dave's grand capabilities. I had a hard time getting my head around how it was that a man, so keen to the most minuscule details of a case, could let his car run out of fluids, or think that tires were good for a million miles a set. He never hesitated to loan it out to me however, so I could look past it.

The lunchtime traffic was going every which way downtown. People coming in for lunch, if they worked beyond, and out for lunch, if they worked within. I would describe my progress toward the police station as abbreviated, despite all opportunities for short cuts and right turns that I made my policy to always utilize. It was a little before noon when I arrived at my destination, and nosed the car in at the front door. Detective Bernard Scott is an easy man to find if you get the description. His was, just under average height, and just over average width. Nothing special there, until you got to his head. He had a big red mustache, and with his hat off, the matching head of hair, made a figurative beacon. I spotted him, coming down the steps in front of the station, on the way to lunch and hurried up behind him.

"What's for lunch, Ben?"

"What's got you so chipper this morning, Trait? Didn't we keep you up long enough last night?"

"Oh, no. Plenty long enough. My typewriter at the office was granted a stay of execution this morning."

"What are you talking about?"

I got the door for him at the corner diner, and he preceded me.

"What I mean, is we've got a client."

"The picture crew?"

"One and the same. Yea, let me get a coffee with cream. The director came in. Wants us to sort out who put the little pellet at the end of that blank. He's hoping that'll be enough to keep his leading man, and hold on to his permits a little longer."

The coffees had come around, and we broke to take a sip. Ben ordered a hamburger, with no cheese, which I admit worried me some. I was sitting there getting ready to ask for favors and information, empathy if you will, from a man that didn't take cheese on a burger. I ordered a ham sandwich. Ben regarded me from the side of his coffee cup.

"So you buy all that, about not believing in guns, do you?"

I shook my head hard for the negative.

"No, sir. I don't have much trust for anybody going around with that sort of opinion of the armaments of our little well regulated militia. I just said that's what this Fishman hopes. I just mean to find out. Did the search of the prop truck turn up anything?"

Supporting the gun is a good way to get most police to like you. It was no acting job on my part either. There are other countries where they throw rocks all the time. Rock throwing, I think, is serious enough that you'd hate to get hit by one, but not so serious as to deter the practice. That's just no way to live, for me.

"We turned the entire prop truck upside down, and inside out. Some of my boys still have a pile of things to process. We have to make sure that Law boy didn't stick the casing in the handle of some sword, or in the padding of a suit of armor."

I shook my head.

"Well, I'm glad you have the staff for all that. Anything turn up in the search of Turner's trailer?"

He picked up his burger and looked at it. I was hoping he'd ask for the cheese he'd forgotten.

"We searched the trailer last night, and went through it again this morning. Nothing more than notebooks and papers. It would have been nice to find a box of .38, but that would make my job too easy.

What else, that Turner made bail as soon as it was posted, you know."

"That's what the director told us. So are you all gonna let them keep shooting? No reason not to, if their talent's out loose."

He tilted his head, and made a sound.

"There're some city council men talking about that today. As it stands now they're shut down, but since no one can leave till after a court appearance, or at least till Turner is cleared, I'm with you. They might as well finish what they're doing. If they're your clients, you might as well talk to them while they're on ice. They're all up above the Williams' restaurant. They rented the whole seventh floor out. Paid the three months in advance. What is it, Jefferson?"

The last part wasn't to me. We were seated side by side at the diner counter, and had been approached by one of the city's uniformed men. He handed a slip of paper to Ben. He wiped his hands, took it, and sent the man on his way.

"Never a lonely moment." I commented.

After scanning it, he folded the slip in half, and passed it to me.

"It's for you."

I took, what was surely a message from Dave, and gave it a read.

It said: John. Finished ledger. Please deliver. Home reviewing film.

I folded it up and stuck it in my coat pocket.

"Did DeGrabber already solve it?" Ben asked.

"Not just yet. By the way, you've got ketchup caught in your mustache." I crammed the last corner of sandwich into processing, gave Ben a pat on the shoulder, and headed out for the car.

My meeting hadn't netted me anything that we didn't already know or expect. I told myself it had been worth doing though, if at least to avoid surprising any of the regulars we should come across. I got to the car quick. First, because it was still freezing, though the sun was out, and from indoors it might have been mistaken for a spring day. And Second, because, on delivery of what would amount to two boxes of paper, I'd receive a check that would keep our little world turning for a few more weeks. That made me think of another idea. Fishman didn't balk at all when Dave hit him up for a home theater, and they had an entire floor of a high rise payed for. That seemed like the sort of client a man can request a draw from, and it not only be given, but expected. Who were 'David and Trait' to let down the wealthy Californians? From the police station downtown, I could see their building. It probably had a bank somewhere in it too, but mine was on the seventh floor. I pointed the car that way, and went.

5

Williams' is one the ritziest spots in town. I had managed to work it into dinner rotation a couple of times on cases, when we've had big time clients, which lately hadn't been often enough. The steaks always came out perfect, and Moe at the white piano, would even sing you one if you passed him some cash. It sat on the ground floor of a tall high rise that housed more of the same in the way of fancy places. A lot of it was hotel, with the lobby and check in on the bottom with the restaurant, and there were some condos, and high priced offices. The seventh floor, where the troupe was staying, was a five bedroom condo.

The condo floors weren't the sort that you just pop up to. They had their own desk and clerk, and their own elevator operator. At the desk they rang up and got me a pass. The elevator opened up to a wide hall, and the door to that floor's living space was front and center. I waited a second to knock. Inside I could hear raised voices.

"You never gave a damn about him or me." It was a woman's voice, in anguish. Another female disputed the accusation.

"You're a fool, Ally. You know damn well I loved him then. Things aren't always meant to be. I understand that. I supported you both, even after all that had happened between us."

That sort of cheese wouldn't have left Detective Scott any room for a patty on his burger. I went ahead and knocked, half hoping that they were just practicing lines, and that everything would switch off when the door opened.

A man, about my age, swung the door wide, as he did, a glass crashed into it, narrowly missing him. He jumped and stepped toward me, out of the line of fire.

I raised my eye brows, and tried to make light.

"Target practice?"

He shot a withering gaze back through the door.

"Are you Mr. Trait?" He sounded like a radio man, but had a face for pictures. I had met him briefly, the night before, and knew him to be Stanley Turner. The gun hating, cop playing, shooter. A conflicted character. I told him I was, and asked to come in. He stood aside, and I crossed the threshold.

It was a swanky place. It had either come furnished or I was going to have to ask for a bigger draw. The rugs were plush, the couches were huge, and the view over the city was first rate. A quick scan of the first big room I was in showed me that the troupe was probably hard on a residence. There were wine and champagne bottles everywhere. Smoke hung low all around. There was a good sized bar in the corner to my left, with a variety of spirits on the bar-top, for easy public access. Men's and women's clothes, and evening attire, lay strewn all around on the backs of chairs, and peeking out as though they'd been kicked under couches. I thought, if this is how the public areas were kept, then the state of the beds and baths, probably meant they wouldn't get their deposit back.

The combatants were known to me, from the night before. The one that had wasted the glass was to my right in a silk nightgown. That was Ally Lawrence. I had seen her in a few pictures. She always struck me as being nice, on film, and in person she looked as good as ever. She was thin, but with a little figure, and her hair was a black bob that framed her face nicely. She had been aiming at Cindy Wilson, the troupe's makeup person. She was nothing to sneeze at herself and had long red hair, which I preferred. She might have been just as good as Ally, or better for all I knew, but having seen one on screen, and all the wonderment that sort of thing carries, I had to give it to the actress. Opportunity for direct comparison, of that sort of thing, never goes well for amateurs.

Ally wasn't acting now. She stood with her shoulders up, and little fists turned out, doing her best to bore a hole through Cindy Wilson's head with her eyes. It had been Cindy that had gotten mushy, and had narrowly avoided the glass, thanks to her close proximity to the door, and Ally's bad aim. While I was making my scan, Stanley took her by the arms, kissed her, and suggested they go for a walk. They headed back out the door.

Now Ally turned her stare at me and asked what I wanted. I told her hello and that I was a big fan, and that I'd come to talk to Fishman. She just pointed to a set of open doors. I took the hint and started that way. She turned toward the bar, presumably to reload for later.

Through the doors was a game room with a pool table. The director was leaned over it trying to bust up a cluster of balls near a corner pocket. He still had on the little scarf, and silly hat, so I resolved to believe that was really the way he went around all the time, and that it wasn't just a director's get up. At the far corner of the table was a man I had only caught sight of. He was sitting on a stool, with a cue in hand, and gave me a nod as I entered.

Fishman hit the cue ball and busted the jam, but didn't make anything. He took a smoke from his mouth, set it on a tray, and gave me his hand.

"Take off your coat and stay awhile, Mr. Trait. Have you met Phillip? He's our costume man."

I got my coat and hat off, and put them in a chair in the corner. Phillip took a shot and missed, and stuck his hand out for me.

"Phillip Spencer." He said, as we shook.

"What brings you by, Mr. Trait? I don't suppose you've had any luck getting my movie back in production."

I shook my head at the director.

"Not so far, sir. If it's any consolation, my friend on the force feels like you all might as well be shooting, since you have to stay in the city anyway. I've come because my partner and I have some operating costs that require liquidity, if we're to help sort this out."

He didn't seem offended, lined up another shot, and asked, "I understand. How much do you need?"

"Five hundred should cover it, sir."

He stepped out of his partner's way, reached into his back pocket for a billfold, and counted out five C's on the spot. I took it from him, as if it were the way it happened everyday, then I just folded it and put it in my pants pocket. I thought it might be a bad look for a moth to fly out of my wallet right then. I figured I had better do some work while I was there.

"Mr. Spencer, I'm going to need to talk to every one in the troupe. Do you mind if I start with you?"

Spencer was probably forty, but didn't look it until you got close. He seemed like a happy guy, and said that would be fine.

"I'll let you two have it. I think there's probably some team building to do out front anyway." With that, Fishman handed me his cue and left us. I strolled over and closed the doors. Spencer was racking for eight ball.

"What kind of things do you want to know, Mr. Trait?" Spencer asked.

I chalked the cue.

"Well, for starters, I'd like to know your opinion, as to whether or not you think Stanley Turner, out there, shot at Mr. Roker, with any foreknowledge of the result."

He stood and leaned on his cue while I broke. I made one, so he talked while I shot.

"It's hard to say. Tempers can get pretty hot around here between the girls, and the men."

"Ah, missed it. Give me an example."

"You heard all that out front, didn't you?"

"I only caught the end. Something about things not working out between Cindy and, I presume, Roker? What did she mean by that?"

"Steve and Cindy, were involved for a little while. Really the entire time we were all in Miami. The men and women shuffle around with each picture and location."

He missed, so I leaned down to go again.

"I was under the impression that Fishman used the same crew for all his pictures."

He looked bashful.

"I guess I didn't explain that very well. I mean they shuffle around with each other."

I tilted my head to one side, and tried not to let on how bad that sounded to me.

"So, what is the state of the union presently?"

"Well, as you may have noticed, we don't have quite even numbers. Right now, at least as of last night, the sleeping arrangements were; Ally Lawrence with the Director, and Cindy with Stanley."

"You make it sound as though alliances can change at any minute. What were they before this?"

I was running the table on him now, so he lit a smoke, and talked between drags.

"In New Orleans, Cindy and I got together. Ally was with Stanley then."

"Did something cause a falling out for Ally to move on to Fishman, or do things just naturally move upward?"

"I don't know what happened. A couple of days after it was announced that Stanley would play the lead in this new one, Ally got all over Walter. That announcement came while we were still in Louisiana. The week before, when we went out, on Bourbon Street, Ally would tell everyone that would listen that she just knew Stanley was going to get to star soon, then when he finally got to, it was like his reward was her leaving him for Walter. He was angry about that, but what could he say?"

"How'd you know he was angry?"

"Cindy told me. He was still sore about it when they started getting involved."

"I see. Then Cindy made her way up the ladder shortly thereafter? I don't mean to sound indelicate."

He frowned as I patted the corner pocket, and sank the eight ball.

"No. You're right. That's probably what it was."

"Tell me some more about Steve Roker. It doesn't sound like he had a partner for this outing."

"Steve had plenty of partners. No one in the troupe since Miami. You can ask Walter his opinion on it, but I think Steve had gotten lazy. During our time in New Orleans, I had to let all his pants and jackets out. He'd stay out till all hours, and bring women back to the house. He's been in a lot of pictures, even before Fishman's, so people recognized him. You want to play another?"

I told him I had some errands to run, but left the door open for further gossip. Nobody was visible in the big room as I went through, so I let myself out, and headed for the ground level. In the elevator I transferred the cash to my billfold. It didn't look like it was going to be anything too taxing for leg work, but Phillip Spencer had made it sound like a mess for motive. I thought my next target might need to be Rob Law, the props man. The police were holding him, because they thought he had disposed of the casing, but since they had let the man that pulled the trigger out with a donation, I figured they'd probably have to cut Law loose soon. Where had that casing gone anyway? We needed that to turn up, preferably on its own. Organically, and not just appear in someone's hand, or on their nightstand.

In that building, you always get valeted, so when I got the car brought to me, I headed for the office. My errand there was uneventful and tedious. Dave had boxed the copies up for me. Two heavy boxes, which was no big deal. The midday traffic was a nightmare, and the lake shore area that the importer was in, was difficult to navigate. I finally made my delivery and got a $150 dollar check for mostly Dave's trouble.

I used the phone on the way out, and rang the police station. I got two pieces of news from the desk sergeant. First, they had released Rob Law back into the wild an hour ago, at two o'clock, for the low low price of one thousand dollars. Fishman had paid it, naturally. Second, the permits for the movie wouldn't have anything decided until Monday. Today was Friday. That didn't surprise me much. City council types, I've found, love to turn a screw when there's some justification. I guess, every now and then, they just want to feel like how senators do all the time. Next I called Dave at his house, and told him we should have a run at Law. He asked me to pick him up, since I had his car anyway. It was another trip through downtown, and back, but I keep a policy of good will toward the car borrowing, and told him I'd be there directly.

Another stuttering trip through downtown, and an only marginally less so jaunt to the last street before suburbia, brought me to Dave's building. His apartment, 303, was a good bit nicer than mine, and often filled me with a curiosity about how he and I split the money, but I never seemed to have any, and he had a separate room to cook in. Ultimately, I believe to each their own, and don't make a big deal about it. Dave's building has a man downstairs, and he buzzed up to tell Dave I was coming. I got in the elevator, went up, and knocked on Dave's door. He said it was open, so I went in.

Well, I tried to go in. As I pushed on the door it stopped against something. Dave said I'd have to squeeze through. Whatever it was against didn't seem very heavy, and I could hear a metallic sound as it scooted out of the way. I came through sideways, making myself as thin as I could with my winter coat on. Dave alway has something going on in his apartment. I can only imagine what the neighbors must think. In its normal configuration it's a good sized sitting room, with a couch, wing backed chair, full bookcase, and stationary desk. The whole thing strikes you as brown when you enter. I had seen it with the sofa stood up against the wall, to make way for a model train set. Arranged as a hostel, for homeless people, one of which had killed somebody. Even temporarily inhabited by cats, which smelled much better than the homeless had. No offense to them. The cat's affinity for self care, as a species, is antithetical to human homelessness.

What had impeded my entry today was a metal stand. Dave was in the floor, on his knees, unpacking a box, and assembling a movie projector on his couch. He affixed an arm to the top of a metal rectangle, and spoke.

"John, could you pass me that screwdriver?"

I looked around. He held his hand out toward me. I finally spotted the screwdriver on the stationary. I tip toed through the parts and packaging, which were strung out on the floor, and wondered how the screwdriver had gotten so far from its point of use.

"I didn't think you liked movies, Dave."

After a second of my holding it there, his hand finally closed, and he applied the screwdriver to the arm.

"I despise them. They're predictable, dramatic, and a poor representation of life."

"They're not all bad."

"The Golden Talon?"

"Well, that one was pretty sorry. It's like anything though, not all the songs are good either. Some paintings don't look like anything at all. We're expected to think that a blue line on a white background, with a baby's pacifier in the corner, has some sort of meaning beyond that the artist ran out of time that day. The movies at least often give us some kind of A to B story. What's the idea getting the Stanley Turner collection anyway?"

He took a large light bulb from some wrapping, and polished at it with his shirt sleeve.

"I want to familiarize myself with his work, and that of the rest of the troupe."

"I'm not sure how much of Turner you're going to see. Roker was the real movie star of the bunch. Well, and Ally Lawrence. I found out that they've all starred for one another, at one time or another."

"Indeed?"

Dave wanted a report so I gave it to him. I told him about my lunch with Scott, my talk with Spencer, and the rest. He didn't seem thrilled that I had taken a draw on the job, but we are partners after all, and I told him it was that or I'd have to hoof it around to talk to our clients. He agreed that that wouldn't look very respectable. I passed him projector parts for another hour, while we kicked around some ideas, and then headed back down for the car. Before we left, Dave called Fishman, and set it up for Law to be at our office at seven. The director said he would send his man. That gave Dave and I just enough time for dinner, so we ate at the diner just a little down from the office.

6

Dave and I go about things differently. I believe my way is good. I'm confident, you see? I think any one that's successful has to believe that what they're doing will work. Otherwise, who's gonna want it? The other key to confidence is being able to see another way, even if it isn't a way you naturally think to go. When I talk to a client, or a suspect, I tend to have conversations. I want to steer it around, in a casual way, and let them tell me things that they want to tell me. I want to make it comfortable. Safe even. What really get's me going, is when someone blabs something they didn't want to tell to anyone, and then their face when they realize what they've done. My best trick is, when that happens, to smile like I know what happened, but that I'll never tell, and keep them comfortable enough to say some more.

Dave did interrogations. Direct concise questions. A lot of questions sometimes. If a suspect clammed up, Dave would start taking guesses. Either the guesses would be right, or so close to right as to make a man feel compelled to straighten it out, or they would be purposely so far out, that he made you think you'd swing if the ideas got out to the street. The damnedest thing about it, and this is why I hardly ever try it his way, is that Dave never came off as mean. He'd ask the hardest, most personal, things he felt he needed to know, just as calmly and professionally as he answered the phone.

Rob Law and Walter Fishman, showed up thirty minutes late for their seven o'clock, in our office. I pulled around a couple of chairs for them at the end of our desks. Fishman was closest to me. He sat shivering from the winter air for the first five minutes. Law looked as if he had raided Spencer's costume truck after his release into society. He had on a big fur that didn't reflect his age, gender, or other stylistic sensibilities. Of course, he wasn't shivering either.

"Explain your duties with the weapons, Mr. Law." Dave asked. He sat turned at his desk, with a leg crossed over the other, and his notepad on his knee.

Law thought for a minute at the best way to start such a broad question. Finally he spoke in a high voice.

"So, I decide, with help from the director here, which gun each character should use in the picture. We consider all sorts of things, from the size of the weapon, to the sort of imagery it carries. Some of the talent have their favorites. Miss Lawrence, for instance, always uses a pearl gripped .32 automatic, whenever a picture calls for her to be armed. She even bought one for her personal use after she starred in,

'The Red Woman'. She played a Russian agent in that and it made some waves."

"I see. Does Stanley Turner have a favorite?"

"Oh, not at all. Just as long as it's a revolver. He doesn't like guns, for some reason, and doesn't want to be asked to do more than point and shoot. With the automatics it can be an exciting shot for the actors to run the slide before a shootout, or reload a magazine. Mr. Turner just prefers not to."

Dave loaded another question.

"Tell, if you would, so that I understand, step by step, what a scene entails, when shots are fired."

Fishman put in there.

"I can probably better answer that. We first rehearse the scene and the lines. They don't have to be very good, because we might move a camera, or change sides of the street. We'll talk about little things there too, like which side someone will stand, or whether a jacket should be buttoned or unbuttoned. Then, once every one knows what they'll say, and where to stand, we call for quiet-"

Law interjected.

"Right before quiet, is when I come out with my pouch, and distribute the weapons. The ones that are going to fire in the scene are readied with blanks. If it's a tight set, I'll hand out cotton for the actors to plug an ear."

Fishman took back the lead.

"Yes, then Douglas calls the scene and take on the board, and cues the start."

"Douglas?" I asked. That was a new name for my notes.

The director explained.

"Yes, Douglas Leech, is the boy that runs our clapper board."

"What's a clapper board?"

"It's a chalk board, with an arm on the top. On the board, the scene and take number is written out by Douglas. Then, as soon as the cameras are rolling, he calls it out and claps the arm, to assist in matching the sound to the picture."

"I see. Then you all shoot the scene, and move on to the next one, unless somebody steps out of a theatre into the shot?"

"That's the plan."

Dave had another.

"How often does someone step into the shot? Are there many interruptions?"

The director shrugged his shoulders at the thought.

"There are constant interruptions, Mr. DeGrabber. First, there's people getting the lines wrong, either objectively, or subjectively. Those are mostly up to myself to determine. There are times, especially filming on site, as we do, that the equipment breaks down and needs resetting. Also, there are stoppages when a car passes by, or even for a sudden gust of wind. Each time, everything must be reset."

"Even the weapons?"

Law took that one.

"Yes, sir. After every take that a blank is used, I reload it. That way we don't lose track of how many rounds we've gone through and waste a good take because the gun was empty when it came time to fire."

"And you deposit the expended blank casings into your pouch immediately after the take?"

"Yes, sir. Especially with Mr. Turner. He likes to get the gun out of his hand so he can smoke. He burns one after every take. I know what you're thinking, because the police have been asking me about it for hours. I never took a live casing out of that .38." He gestured toward me. "When you found me, in my trailer, I was searching my pouch and everything, to make sure I hadn't taken out a spent casing without noticing. It wasn't there. I can't say where it came from, short of the box of blanks having a live round in it, and even then everybody can tell the difference between the round nose of a bullet, and the pointed crimping of a blank cartridge."

"How was the scene, that John interrupted, supposed to go, Mr. Fishman?", Dave asked.

Fishman had warmed up a bit, and loosened his thin scarf.

"Stanley was playing a hard boiled detective. His smoking worked well for that, and Steve was the mob boss that Stanley's character was after. We were shooting one of the final scenes first, you see. We'd gotten a lot of the inside work done in offices, and hotel lobbies, even at the police station. The scene that you interrupted, was supposed to have come after a chase through the streets and theatre. At the mouth of the alley, it was all supposed to culminate in a quick draw moment. Steve was to wheel around, and say some short lines, and raise his pistol to shoot Turner, but Turner would be quicker on the draw, and shoot him before he got the chance. Then, Turner was supposed to finish the villain off as he lay there on the ground."

"Who's idea was the coup de gras, Mr. Fishman? It proved to be a convincing performance."

"Yeah, shooting a guy on the ground doesn't sound much like good guy stuff." I added.

Fishman paid no mind to Dave's gallows humor.

"I'm not sure who first suggested it. It's meant to be a hard and gritty detective film, you see. It had been in the script for a couple of weeks, throughout the planning for the chase scene, at least."

I hadn't looked away from our guests, but I became aware that Dave had spotted some action in our hallway. It was starting to get late, so Sid must have gone home for the night. Dave sat his pad down on the desk, brushed back his perpetually messy hair, and started toward the door. Halfway across there came a hard knock. I could tell right away it was the police, with their patented, open up or else, brand of rapping.

Dave swung the door open, and Ben Scott entered in a huff. He brought two uniformed men in behind him.

"Mr. Law, we need you at the station for further questioning." Ben commanded with authority.

Law looked both young and silly, in his big fur. He sank into his chair, looking defeated.

Dave tried to help.

"Mr. Law was just helping to answer our questions about this unfortunate slaying. He surely hasn't loaded any additional weapons while under our eye."

Ben had a hand on Law's shoulder, and was getting him up. He gave us a friendly answer, that he didn't have to give.

"We've been up to the seventh floor condo, with a warrant. We found $500 dollars cash hidden in a single shoe, on a top closet shelf, in Law's room."

Law's voice was higher than ever to launch his protest.

"So I've got some savings. That's not a crime."

"It's a crime if it was payment to stick a real bullet in Turner's piece. Let's head down to the station so you can tell us how you saved it all up."

I thought about telling Law, that unless he was under arrest, he didn't have to go with Scott, but the thing was ticklish. He was out on bail, and tentatively charged with some level of manslaughter. He had also been spotted playing with the evidence right after the killing. Maybe if he had wore his own overcoat around I might have believed he'd have half a grand sitting in surplus, but the way he looked standing there in his big fur, he just didn't cut the sort of figure that instilled you with a lot of confidence in his decision making. The other thought I had was about how I was sitting there with five C's in my billfold too, and the man that had put them there was sitting across from me, having just that day found another thousand to get Law out. If you wanted to follow the money, you didn't have far to go. I kept quiet, so they wouldn't take Fishman too, and they led Law out and down to a waiting squad car.

Fishman had gotten up and stood looking rattled. He asked if there was something we could do, and Dave let him down easy that we couldn't. He left after a short monologue about his general worry for his friends, and his film.

With the room now clear, I returned the chairs to their proper place along the wall, and put four of the five hundreds in my safe; Dave had bought a matching set of small safes for the office, so we each had one on our respective sides of the room. Dave was sitting back at his desk, with a finger on his nose looking thoughtful. He spoke when he had decided on something.

"I'm going to go home and finish putting the projector screen together. The films are supposed to arrive tomorrow around noon. See if you can find this Ally Lawrence, and learn more about the troupe's personal relations."

I flipped to tomorrow's page on the schedule sheet.

"What time would you like to have her in? The morning, before your pictures get here?"

Dave slid his chair back, stood up, and righted the lapel on the dark blue jacket he always wore, and said,

"I hoped you would find her tonight."

"Sure thing, Boss." I grinned and went back to my safe to get one of the hundreds back. No telling what sort of liquidity would be needed to take a Hollywood starlet out. With that, we shut the lights off and closed shop for the night.

7

Dave took his car back with him to the house, because he would need it in the morning to pick his films up, as the postman had told him it was too much to bring by, unless he wanted to wait a little longer. That left me to call a cab. I got in a booth and called the depot. My favorite driver, Ralph, was working downtown, it being Friday night, so I had to settle for whoever they'd send me. From the booth I spotted any old cabbie, told them not to worry about it, and waved him down.

Heading toward downtown, I started thinking where Ally Lawrence might be on a cold Friday night, with no movie to shoot anytime soon. After the dust up I had witnessed with Cindy Wilson, I didn't figure they were all sat around the condo playing charades. Also, from the little bit I'd heard, she was taking the passing of her former boyfriend and co-star, pretty hard. That meant that she was likely out holding her sorrows under some small puddle of liquid, until the bubbles stopped. The question was where. I tried to put myself in her shoes. Good, expensive shoes. Where would I go, downhearted, beautiful, wealthy, and recognizable? I admit, they weren't attributes that I ever had the luxury to consider, so I just decided to go where I would go, given the same circumstances. That would have me, allowing for unfamiliarity of the area, at Joe's Place. It was a little hole in the wall, walking distance from her building, that did a fair amount of business, where they kept the lights low, and Joe wouldn't ask you many questions, unless you really looked like you wanted them. So that's where I would be.

I told the cabbie to take me to the Stiletto instead. Ally Lawrence isn't John Trait. Stiletto, is a hot spot, where the drinks are criminally overpriced, that the wealthiest, most influential people in Chicago, good or bad, went to get loosened up. It was on the top floor of a high rise, and included a roof top bar, that overlooked Lake Michigan. The rooftop was closed during the winter months, on account of the way your eye lashes would freeze in the wind.

"Would you like me to wait, sir?" The cab driver asked as I got out.

"No, sir. I'm likely to have a late one, if I have one at all." I counted out some bills, and he got on his way.

In and out from under the awning, came all kinds of well heeled people. I recognized a few prominent business owners, and their wives, as well as a couple of underworld operators. The latter were accompanied by multiple women, certainly not wives, and not too discrete security details.

I took the elevator to the top floor, and had to pay two bucks just to get in. I parted with it, and kept my grumble to myself. A boy at coat check held his hand out, and I was lightened another single. With the floor tax paid, I gave it a once over.

It was a fantastic spot. The decor was primarily a deep red, and it had become a custom for the female guests to coordinate with it. The tables were too little to eat off of, but that was no problem. Most people only sat for breaks from the large dance floor, which was under a crystal chandelier. It was nearly full. Beyond the floor, they had a full band playing, in merlot colored jackets, behind shimmering silver stands.

I didn't see Ally Lawrence right away, but did spy a member of the troupe to my right in a corner booth. It was Stanley Turner. He was by himself. He looked as good as you'd expect a movie star to, in a black tuxedo that he wore classy, without looking overbearing. He was smoking, as he had been advertised to, and by the look of the tray at his hand, he had been for a little while. I made my way over to him.

"Anybody sitting here?"

"I guess you are. Trait, isn't it?" He seemed down in the mouth, but despite that, each time I heard him speak, I wanted to look around and see who had turned on the talk radio. I told him he had the name right, and sat down. He had more to say. "You come here too, Trait?"

"No, only on the job, if it calls for it. Yeah, let me

57

get what he's having."

Turner gulped the last half of his drink down, and asked for another also. Good scotch with two ice cubes. He specified.

"Did you come looking for me?"

"I thought I'd find Miss Lawrence here, actually. No offense."

He grinned. Like a movie star.

"Well, you found her." He had a fresh drink up for a sip, and pointed a finger. I followed it, and it led my eyes to the bar. As I looked that way, an older man moved over, and I saw her.

Ally Lawrence either didn't know the tradition of the red dress, or had purposely meant to buck it. She had on a kind of modernized take on a flapper dress. Silver sequins, knee length, and tighter around the middle. She sparkled like a billboard sign, there at the bar. A narrow, sensual billboard sign. She had formed quite a congregation around her too. Right now, she was leading the group, with her martini glass high in the air, and getting everyone else to do likewise. It was the sort of sorrow drowning, by way of revelry, I had expected.

I took the scene in for a moment, and made a glance back toward my company. Stanley Turner had a look of mild disgust on his face, and his big jaw clamped tight. I put on a tone, that I hoped would say I agreed with his sentiments.

"It doesn't look like Miss Lawrence is going to have much time to chat."

He took another big drink, and finished his cigarette.

"No, Ally doesn't have a lot of time for much lately. Not much beside partying, and Fishman." He pulled a pack of smokes from his breast pocket and lit one.

"Does Fishman support that kind of thing? He doesn't really strike me as the wild type."

"I don't know what Fishman supports. It's not a real thing like what we had."

"Tell me a little bit about that. I heard you two got together in New Orleans. Was it serious?"

He took a long drag, and another big gulp of scotch. I held mine to my lips to try to show I was with him, but since I had work to do, thought it best not to try to keep up. To be honest, I don't know if I could have anyway.

"That wasn't the first time we'd gotten together. Ally and I grew up in the same town, together. Back in Oregon. We saw each other off and on through school, and then she went off to L.A., and I went to the Air Force."

I took the opportunity to make friends, and told him I'd been in the Army myself. It wasn't much, with the way branch rivalries go, but it was better than nothing. I was half surprised he didn't think I was trying to patronize him, my team being the real fighters of the campaign and all, but we clinked our glasses, and he continued his story.

"Anyway, when I got back, I moved to Hollywood also, and got back to acting. I contacted her as soon as I got to town, and she turned me on to some opportunities, and I've worked steady ever since. We'd see each other at parties, and the odd movie set. Then, when Fishman came up with this idea to shoot his movies on site, he got Ally, and she suggested he bring me along. That was a few years ago now. We had a relationship for a good while, probably two years, while we traveled around doing these pictures for Fishman."

"Then I guess you guys fell out?"

He made a kind of annoyed smirk, but kept talking.

"I don't know what happened. She went back to Hollywood, during a break, and made a couple other pictures, and the next thing I knew, she wrote me a letter saying we should probably see other people, but keep working together. The next time I saw her was when we all got to Miami for, 'Miami Heat'. Did you see that one?" I told him I hadn't, so he gave me a rundown. "It was about an abusive husband, played by Roker, and a girl fighting back to escape him. That was Ally, of course. I played the other man that she falls in love with at the end. The irony of the thing seemed to be lost on them though."

"The irony is lost on me too, pal."

He crushed out the last of his smoke, and reached in for the pack again. He raised his voice some.

"That damn Roker. He was an abuser. I mean, not the sort to slap anyone around, but it was the way he played with them." The waiter was back. "Yeah, same thing. Thank you." He passed off his glass and told some more of what happened.

"We were in Miami shooting the movie. The weather was wonderful. We all looked great in the light. The whole crew was showing up to work in shorts and swim wear. Ally and Roker were joined at the hip."

I put in there.

"Now, I was under the impression that Roker was with Cindy Wilson in Miami."

"That's the damn thing. Roker tried to be with everyone. Toward the end, Cindy was his main one, but I'll get to how that happened."

He was sure wide open now. He got his fresh drink, and I had made it to the bottom of mine, so I refilled too. We were keeping the waiter on a steady trot. The stories were coming my way easy. I kept quiet and listened.

"So, we were nearly through with 'Miami Heat', and were a full week ahead of schedule. The weather took a turn, so we couldn't film the last few scenes. Fishman decided to take a few days and fly back to

L.A., to meet with some executives about the marketing. They were having trouble with how they were going to sell a movie about a man beating his wife."

I felt like we had become good enough friends to risk a comment, so I did.

"Yeah, what kind of pictures is Fishman trying to make anyway?"

Turner shook his head.

"He has this idea that Hollywood is too clean, and that none of it feels real enough. I don't agree with all the things he has us do on film, but he has good backing, and the work is steady. The traveling is nice too, even though it can be a pain when he get's the idea that he needs to shoot in Chicago in the dead of winter. I don't know how you all live here, like this."

We talked about that kind of thing, for a little while, and then I got him steered back to the Miami job.

"So, Fishman left that night, and the next day Steve told us he had chartered a skiff to take us over to Havana. None of us had ever been, so it was exciting. When we got there it was a first class party. They had everything you could ask for. Illegal stuff too. I think that's where Ally was turned on to her habit."

We were getting into stuff I thought I could use now. I took a sip of my drink, and tried not to act excited.

"What sort of habit?"

The whole time he had been talking, he hadn't really taken his eyes off Ally and the bar. He pointed the finger again.

"You see that bracelet she has on, with the wide top?"

I told him I did.

"It's a compartment."

We were at a distance, but now I was aware of a few more of the tell-tale signs of a regular nasal sort of habit. She rubbed her nose a bit more than you'd ever expect, with it being the middle of winter, and there not being a speck of pollen in the air anywhere. I could also just make out that the nail on her small right hand finger, was manicured to be a good bit longer than the others.

"You think Roker did that?"

Turner scoffed.

"I know he did that. It was his whole trick. Sure women want to be around guys in pictures. That's easy enough, but still, a lot of women will only go so far. I appreciate that too, mind you. I think it shows some character. Roker didn't like it, and would use that powder to close the deal. Not everybody can handle that stuff. It sticks to them. Ally hasn't been the same since."

"Well then how did you pull her away from him in New Orleans."

"We still had another couple of weeks of filming in Miami, after the Cuba trip. Apparently, anything you could have in Cuba, you can get in Miami, without much more trouble. She kept getting further and further out, till one night I confronted her about it. She felt bad, and wanted to get help. She told Roker they were through. He didn't really seem to mind, and moved on to Cindy."

Ally was coming across toward us now. A couple of men pulled at her arm, but she brushed them off, and told them she had to go. You could tell by the way she flashed them smiles and winks, that she was an old hat at dealing with the adoring public. Her walk wasn't exactly graceful though. She asked if Turner would watch her drink while she went to freshen up. He said he would. She left, and he talked to me a bit more.

"I'm going to head home, Trait, since you need to talk to her anyway. You think you can get her back to the condo in one piece for me? She gets indignant with me if I try to help."

I told him I'd keep a lookout for him, and he got up and made his way out. I was surprised he was as steady on his feet as he was. The waiter came back by, and I ordered a refill, and one of whatever Ally had been drinking. The drinks, and my actress, made it back to the table at about the same time.

"Where did Stanley go?" She had a pleasing voice.

"He said he needed to turn in. Fishman sent me to

talk to you about the other night."

She lowered her shoulders like a kid that's been told it's time to leave the fair. She sat down anyway, and took a sip of the purple drink I had for her.

"I'm sorry you had to see me like that earlier, Mr. Trait. Cindy has it in her head that I wanted that to happen to Steve. Can you believe she'd think something so terrible as that?"

I started to wonder if all the women I might interact with on this case, were going to talk as if someone had wrote it into a script. Of course, I just told her that I couldn't believe it, and asked why she thought that, which is what she wanted me to do in the first place.

She took another drink and gave her take.

"Cindy thinks, since I left Steve in Miami, that he might as well have been dead to me, but that can't be further from the truth. Steve opened up a whole new world to me. To my mind and body. Our love was just a fire that burned too hot to sustain, you see. So I had to leave him. Stanley showed me that. Had Steve and I stayed together, we might have just burned up."

Do you ever hear something so ridiculous, at least in the way it comes out, that you feel squeamish? That bit about fire, and whatnot, had me trying to hide the fact that I wanted to sink down under the table with some kind of embarrassment by proxy. After hearing what little I had from Cindy Wilson on the matter, the idea was probably sound, as far as they were all concerned. The thought about what Dave would make of that kind of melodramatic logic, and the look on his face, which I imagined to be one of total bewilderment, caused me to hide a giggle, which was easier than the embarrassment.

I told her, "I understand Miss Lawrence- Ally. I understand, Ally. So what about Mr. Fishman? No worries about combustion there?"

She waved a hand, and answered with enthusiasm.

"Oh, Mr. Trait- John. That's what I love so much about Walter. He's an older and wiser man. He understands what I need, and makes sure I get it. John, I love this song. Dance with me."

With that, she grabbed me by the wrist and led me out onto the floor. It was crowded. I don't mind crowds so much. It's the people bumping into me, that I find grating. Usually I only dance when absolutely necessary, but I couldn't pass up the chance to dance with a well known actress, even if what I had learned about her had knocked a bit of sheen off of her in my eyes.

She was a good close dancer. There was no doubt about that. Though the song we'd gotten out there to was made to sound like a special case, she kept me upright for the next four. The band was first class, and the lights off the chandelier made for an elegant atmosphere. We talked a little as we danced.

"Have you ever thought about acting, John?" She had her head on my shoulder as we swayed to a slow one.

"Oh, no, Ally. I'm not a very good liar, so I don't see how I'd ever pull that off."

She made a giggle and turned her eyes up slightly to meet mine.

"It's not about lying, John. It's about getting into the mind of somebody else. You detectives do that all the time, don't you? Besides, more than that, it's about what you look like. You could stand to be a little taller, but still I have to look up at you, and your dark eyes and hair would be great. I like the way you comb it, a bit to the side, like that. Let me see your chin." She took my chin by her thumb and forefinger and turned my head to see the profile. "Pretty strong, John Trait.", was her critique.

It made me feel bashful, so I tried to change the subject. We danced and talked some more, but mainly just about the place and the band. When we finally started back to the table, it had been claimed by a party of six. They were the underworld types and had a sentry at the table's edge, so I decided they could keep it. Looking at my watch, it read a bit after one, so I suggested we make our way into a cab, and call it a night. She played the pouty toddler role again, but obliged.

At her building, I got out of the cab, and told the driver to wait while I walked her up. She said she wasn't ready to go up, and that we should have some drinks at Williams'. I had predicted it would be a late night, so I told the cab to go on. Williams' was of similar social standing as the Stiletto, but it had a black and white decor, and a more, sit down and talk low, sort of energy.

We got into a corner booth, and Ally ordered a bottle of good champagne. I was about out of ideas, having learned so much of the company relations from Turner, so I decided to turn my attention to more technical inquires.

"So, Ally, Bob Law told me you have a favorite prop gun. Have you ever had anything, like what happened to Turner and Roker, happen to you?"

She had been to the ladies room as soon as we'd entered and was way up. She answered excitedly.

"No, John. I never have. I do love the shooting and things though. It's so fun. I used to tell Stanley, that if he'd just get an automatic, like this." She reached into a small purse and pulled out the pearl gripped .32 I had heard about.

"Whoa, Ally. Let's not take that out in public." I got my hands on it and worked it back into her bag. No sooner than I let go, her hand popped back up with it. She laughed as she spoke, and waved it around.

"It's ok, silly. This is the prop one. See?"

Well now she had done it. My ears rang, and the piano player stopped. The whole place froze, and looked in our direction. As though it had held time still, she released the trigger, and so put everyone back into motion. She addressed the room, loudly, that they were just blanks, but the patrons didn't seem to think it had been as fun as she did. I covered my face with my hands, this time making no attempt to hide my embarrassment.

A man appeared from a kitchen door, clearly the manager of the house, and approached us in a huff. I gathered Ally up, and tried to apologize as we slid out of the booth. I pulled the pistol out of her hand and stuck it in my jacket pocket for safe keeping. The manager didn't even give me time to pay for our drinks. He shoved me in the back, which I didn't hold against him at all given the circumstance, and got us out the door.

"I think it's time you went home, Miss Lawrence. Right now. You'll be lucky if they don't call the police and arrest you for that."

She laughed heartily, and tried to tell me I was being too serious. I was sore, so I pulled her along to the condo elevator. By the time we'd gotten into the elevator, she had decided to be sore too, and stood with her arms crossed in what I believed to be a wholly indefensible huff of her own. When the doors opened up on the seventh floor, she turned her nose up at me, and strode to the condo door, knocked, and was let in.

"Good night, Mr. Trait." She nearly shouted back

to me, and slammed the door to.

I shook my head and pressed the button to get back to ground level. I thought about going in and trying to smooth things over at the restaurant, being that it's one of my favorite places to eat, but decided it was probably too fresh a wound. I went out and hailed a taxi. This time I happened to get Ralph. My favorite. I got in.

"How's it going, John? Having a good night?"

I settled into the back seat.

"I've been dancing with a famous Hollywood actress. After doing it, I'm saddened to report, that I don't recommend it. Take me to the house, will ya?"

Without giving up anything that I thought might ever need to come up in court, I gave Ralph a cursory report of the evening. He had a good laugh about it, which made me feel better. It was late and traffic wasn't bad, so I made it home in no time.

Emptying my pockets, I remembered that I still had Ally's pistol with me. I gave it a once over. It was some kind of German design. Nickel plated and polished to shine. It fit in the palm of your hand, and I could see how it would look good for a woman in a movie. I popped the magazine out and made a worrying discovery. If the shot she fired off in the restaurant had been a blank, then it had been the only blank in the gun. I stared down at the magazine with my hand over my mouth, at the little round bullets within, and shook my head at it. She might have killed somebody. Herself, or maybe me. That put me on to some more questions. Had someone swapped out her personal gun, for the prop, or did she just lie about the blanks and want to make a scene. Maybe she had mixed the guns up herself, and it was all just an honest mistake. Just think of the calamity it would have been though, if they thought this was the prop gun, and the real bullets had been fired on set. Finally, the police hadn't found Rob Law to have a box of real .38 in his possession, but it seemed Ally had the means to load her .32, if she had wanted to. Tomorrow we would have to look into the troupe's personal weapons, if they had any. I set all that in another box in my mind, for now, and went to bed.

8

The next day, I made it to the office bright and early. The sun was out, but it was still well below freezing. I grabbed a paper on the way, and glanced at the headlines. No report of any actresses shooting up downtown. Good news. Dave wasn't in the office but had been, so his nearly perfect streak of preceding me to work continued. I knew because he had left a couple of messages on our pad.

The first, was a note about a call he'd gotten to take a look around for some stolen yard ornaments. I looked up the name on the note in the phone book, and found the address to be lucrative. I called and set up to take a look at three o'clock. The other message was from Dave to me. It said that his films had arrived, and that he would be viewing them. Presumably, he would go till he got done. I'll be honest, it seemed like a strange use of his time. I had more names on my list. A few more of the primary acting troupe, and then there were guys like Douglas Leech, the clapper, and probably some other ancillary persons, that needed going over. It might have been good for Dave to get around to some of them, but he had pulled his weight on all our cases before, and I expected he would here too, by the time it was all said and done. I called the taxi depot, for Ralph, also.

Hanging up the phone, I got a knock at the office door. The height and build told me who was calling, so I invited him in. It was Ben Scott again. This time he'd come for a solo performance, and didn't look any more upset than I expected him to, given that his murder investigation was fully snagged.

"How's the weather, officer?"

He took one of the chairs from the wall, and swung it around to the end of my desk. He folded down into it like an old man. Ben wasn't any older than Dave and I. Not wet behind the ears, by any means, but far from our anatomy being in disagreement on sitting and standing. I think he just liked to look the part of the grizzled inspector. He stroked his red mustache, and spoke.

"It's damn cold, Trait."

Now, with what was very small talk, out of the way, I asked some things.

"Did you find out where Law came across that five hundred dollars?"

"He said it was a bonus, from Fishman. We got Fishman in separately, and he suggested it was Law's savings."

"That's not a good look for Fishman."

"It doesn't sit well for either of them. We've got a real problem though with this casing."

"Still no sign of it?"

He shrugged.

"You were there that night. We had the whole night crew, and a couple of the lab men, called in, working that search. We searched all the people, even the women, and all their trailers. Yesterday, I sent men with magnets down the drains and culverts looking for it in the water down below street level. They could have left the magnets up top, because there was ice down at the bottom. The district attorney says we need the casing to come up in some sensible person's hand, or else the whole thing may as well be an act of God. A confession would work too, but I think to get that, that would require an act of God. Between you and me, I don't think the D.A.'s given it a lot of thought. Even if we find the casing, we're not gonna know who put it in the gun and who took it out. I'd bet, if it showed up, they'd all point at each other, or say it got there on its own feet. Help me out this time, do you and DeGrabber have anything?"

I'd listened with a somber look on my face, hoping that he might confide some useful piece, that I could tie onto the strings I was holding, but the revelation that he was as stuck as he'd been at the start wasn't anything either of us could use. I did want to help him though, and Fishman hadn't said we couldn't use the officials to sort it out.

"I tell you what, I need to make a report to Dave anyway. He's at the house going through all of Turner and Fishman's films."

Scott showed me his hands, and asked,

"What for?"

I lifted my shoulders.

"I have no idea, but you might as well come with me and sit in on it. Only fair, since you volunteered yours."

"Alright, I'll drive."

"I already have my favorite cabbie en route. He'd be sore if I sent him back without a fare. You can ride with me, and then you can run me downtown, when we get back here."

That worked for him. Before we left, he used my phone to tell the station where they could find him, should there be a break, then I locked up and we headed down. Ralph rolled up as we stepped out.

"John, you're really falling off from that actress you told me about."

"Actress? What's he talking about, Trait?"

We got settled in, and on our way. I explained the dig. As I gave Ben the who and the where, Ralph spilled the incident with the firecracker at Williams'. Ben got sore about the discharging of a firearm, blank or not, inside a restaurant for the affluent. He took it personal, as the police are trained to do. I told him I did all I could. I also began to wonder why Ralph was my favorite driver, but then I don't often share cabs with police detectives, so his indiscretion was probably not going to be a problem very often.

Ben had never been to Dave's house, and was impressed by the quality of neighborhood we'd arrived in. We made our way up to 303 and knocked on the door. Dave signaled that it was open, and again the door only came open a crack. This time the obstruction was much more solid, and Ben and I had to remove our overcoats and pass them through to fit. Once we got in, with no small difficulty on Ben's part, we saw what we were up against.

Dave had his couch pulled around nearly up against the door. In such orientation, it spanned nearly the entire width of the room. In the middle of the couch, just in front, stood the projector on its stand, now fully assembled and in operation. Beyond that, and entirely blocking the passage to Dave's kitchen, was a large slick silver screen. The whole place was now a theatre, and strictly a theatre. Dave had only bothered to get up as far as to take our coats through the crack in the door. He had tossed them in a heap to one side of the room, and was back on the right side of the couch, as we entered.

"Where are we gonna sit?" Ben asked. He was trying not to be too incredulous, but I could tell the arrangement had given him cause to wonder about Dave. Sometimes, I forget that I've had a couple of years to get used to Dave's transforming home. I always imagined Ben's house, which at the time I hadn't been to, to be a picture of order and cleanliness, which it was. Now, as I made my way around the couch, and in front of the projector, I saw that Dave had the other two dozen or so film cans on the other end, making his home largely a single seater. I looked around and pulled the wing backed chair out of Dave's bedroom, offered it to Ben, and he took it. I leaned against the book shelf, for now.

"Detective Scott, it is good to host you finally." Dave said that as if Ben wasn't looking at him, and the apartment, as if he had two heads.

I explained Ben's accompanying me, then Ben gave his bleak report again. I began mine with a little preamble about how Ben was being taken into the fold on this, and that within reason, he'd have to set his cop hat aside, should anything be reported that could be deemed unscrupulous, or generally frowned upon by justice. He agreed to my terms, citing his sole and primary rationale as the fact that he had already come in the door, so I began. Dave and Scott both, were very interested in Ally Lawrence's recreational habits, as well as her pistol. I had brought the pistol with me. They both inspected it.

"So, there may be a slug in the ceiling of Williams'?"

I answered Ben's question with sympathy. You'd have thought his dog had knocked over his favorite coffee cup, by the way he sounded hurt.

"Could be. They're short payment on a bottle of good champagne too." Now to Dave. "So what do you hope to find in all these films?"

Dave sat low in his couch with his arms crossed and his legs out in front of him. If you didn't know his mannerisms you would have thought he had paid no attention, but I knew he hadn't missed a syllable. He made no move, but gave a type of answer.

"I'm not certain. I've only had time enough to watch one, but I plan to go through them all without delay. Some of Mr. Fishman's films, by their synopses, include some provocative subject matter. I know you reported that Mr. Turner said he had good backers, but I imagine they are not of the film industry proper. Also, I plan to try to decide if there's truth to Turner's claim that he is totally ignorant about the function of firearms. Lastly, I hope to be able to determine what level of thespians Mr. Fishman's troupe are. One may be acting for us in all of our meetings, and we can't know without a baseline."

I nodded my head. It sounded as good as anything else we had learned, being that nothing we had so far looked to get us any closer. Ben grunted. I got the impression that Ben didn't feel like he had much use for establishing performance baselines. He had told me before that he sometimes felt, as an official arm of justice and public order, that he functioned much like a hammer. Smashing down rouges and evil doers swiftly, and without prejudice. He'd spoken, as romantically as a man of his disposition may, about a desire to use the sort of light touch, or clever angles, that Dave and I had the luxury to employ. This movie watching was a bridge too far though. He got up and tried to pace around, but finding the arrangement to be not conducive to it, announced that he needed to get back downtown. Dave reiterated that he didn't yet have anything to contribute, so I got up to go too. Ben tossed our overcoats back out through the crack in the door, and onto the hallway carpet, and began to squeeze through when a voice in the hall called to him by name, and asked if everything was alright. Ben wriggled through, and grabbed his coat up. I was close behind.

Coming up the hall were two of Ben's coworkers.

"What's going on?" Ben asked, shooting an arm down his coat sleeve.

The smaller of the two responded,

"Sir, we've come to report that the casing has been found."

I'd just reached down and retrieved my coat from the floor, when Dave slid out behind me, much more smoothly than I would have expected.

"Who presented it?" He asked.

The officers looked from Dave, to their boss. Ben motioned them to go ahead.

"Phillip Spencer, sir."

"Impossible."

"Why impossible, DeGrabber?" Ben sounded irritated.

Dave ignored him.

"Where did Spencer claim he discovered this casing?"

"In the coat pocket of Stanley Turner, sir."

Now Ben nearly shouted, "We searched him head to toe, and the whole costume truck. Who missed it? Was it Peterson?"

"Mr. Spencer said he found it in one of Turner's personal jackets, that he had in his room. Spencer thinks he must have kept the casing from us, and hid it there after the search. We've sent men to bring Turner in."

Ben was calming down. "Let's go then."

I jumped in.

"Detective Scott, Fishman hired us to sort this thing out, and hopefully clear his leading man, so that, in a way, makes Turner our client. Don't you think we should be there?"

Ben was eying Dave. I figured he was thinking something along the line of, why do you have to rain on my parade, and why do you always have to be right. Dave was standing in the hall, with his arms crossed looking at the floor. I guess he was looking at the floor, though we couldn't see his eyes on account of his unkept hair. It was a position for standing thinking that I'd seen many times. Ben regarded him for a moment, and then motioned for us to follow. As we all four started down the hall, Dave dove back through the crack in the door, and shot back out with his grey overcoat in hand.

Dave and I rode together downtown, in Dave's car. We tried to follow behind the official's vehicle, but it was clear that they drove with the security that no one was likely to turn lights on and comment on how fast they went. Even without any fringe benefits, we weren't far behind in arriving at the station house.

Ben had waited in the police station lobby for us, and led us down a hall on the first floor. He opened a door that said, Interrogation A, on a little black panel. I half expected to see Stanley Turner there, cuffed to a metal table, with a hot lamp in his face. That sort of set up must have been further down the hall, in Interrogation B, or C, maybe. This was a conference room with a long table, six respectable looking chairs, and a rolling black board pushed up against the far wall. Maybe for the suspect to draw maps of where he hid the bodies, or at least his best guess at where they'd be, if he could somehow put himself in the bad guy's shoes. That item seemed strange to me.

Turner was there, in shirt sleeves, on the far side of the table from the door. His jacket was hung behind him on his chair, so he must have gotten in there under no great duress. He still had his smokes too, and again the remaining capacity of his ash tray told how long he'd been waiting. I counted six butts, which for him wasn't too long a sit.

We took seats. Ben and I opposite of Turner. Dave positioned himself on Turner's side of the table, with a chair between them. He turned it a bit to get a look at all of us.

"Mr. Turner, my officers said you came along peacefully to talk with us today. That is appreciated. Hopefully we can get all this sorted out, and have you back to the condo before too long." Ben was more friendly than I had expected him to be. I had never had the pleasure to fly around the walls of his interrogation room, so it was unclear to me if his cordiality was a function of Turner's standing, or if he just liked to ramp up as he went.

Turner seemed unconcerned. He blew some smoke, and spoke dryly.

"You all have us held here in the cold. We can't work, and we can't leave. Seems like we don't have much choice but to do what you say."

Ben frowned and decided he had been friendly enough for the morning. He reached into his coat pocket, and pulled out a small yellow envelope. He emptied its contents as he spoke.

"We have found this .38 shell casing, that we believe launched the bullet that killed your coworker, Steve Roker." The brass tingled onto the table, and came to rest on its side. Ben took it carefully with two fingers, and stood it up on its end.

I watched Turner closely, trying to see a crack. There was nothing at all. Less than nothing. It made me think that Dave's idea about acting baselines wasn't so kooky after all. Then Turner gave an answer that struck me as lazy. Sloppy even.

"What's that? I've told you all I don't know weapons."

Ben shook his head at him.

"Mr. Turner, we requisitioned your file from the Air Force. Though you were an abject failure as a marksman, to claim total ignorance of these things, would be foolhardy. Do you have any idea where this one came from?"

Turner moved his head back, and raised his brows, took a drag of his cigarette, and looked exactly like a man that had no good guess.

"I don't have any idea, officer. Did it have any fingerprints on it?"

Ben was undeterred. He leaned his chair back on its legs, reached over his head to the door, and knocked. Instantly, the door opened, and a uniformed officer brought in another package. This bundle was about the size of a toaster, and was wrapped in paper. Ben untied a string around it, and exposed a navy blue sport coat. He laid it out on the side of the table.

"When was the last time you wore this jacket, Mr. Turner?"

"I'm not sure. I've been trying every one I own,

and any in Phillip's costume trailer that will fit, to try and get ahead of the cold you all have here. I think I took that one from the trailer some time early this week. Why?"

Ben picked up the casing again, with his thumb and forefinger, and held it out above the table. He explained.

"Mr. Turner, we found this .38 brass. In the pocket of this jacket. Do you have any idea how it might have gotten in there?"

"May I see that, Mr. Scott?" Dave had been sitting with his arms crossed, staring at the casing. Ben shot him an impatient glance and slid the casing down.

Dave took it up, and held it up to the light. He brought it close to his face and sniffed of it too. After a good look, still holding it, he asked Turner,

"You don't recall any gunshots downtown, do you Mr. Turner?"

Turner thought for a moment, or at least he acted like he was thinking. At this point I was starting not to trust my own eyes with him.

"I don't believe so. Ally said she had fired a shot at the bottom of our building. That's what she told us when she got in last night, but I didn't hear it. Is it from that gun she keeps in her bag?"

"I did not suppose you had. And no, Ally Lawrence's sidearm is of a different caliber, but as you've stated, you don't know weapons, do you." Now Dave swung his eyes over to me. "John, do you have your revolver with you?"

"No, I had Miss Lawrence's .32, so I left it at the office."

Dave frowned.

"Mr. Scott, one of your officers must have one available to us."

Ben reached in toward his breast pocket, and pulled out his own Smith & Wesson.

"I've got one right here. What are you getting at DeGrabber?" He slid the pistol over, not as carefully as I like a loaded gun to be handled, and Dave took it.

He flipped the cylinder out, and turned the gun toward the ceiling. Turner's jacket was on that side of the table, so the rounds fell quietly out of their holes, and onto it. Now with the chambers emptied, Dave took the spent casing, and set it into one. He held it by the rim and released it. The brass dropped all the way down, flush into battery, ready to close and fire, if it had been a loaded one. Dave held the cylinder steady with his other hand, and jostled the whole gun. You could hear the brass rattle around, ever so lightly, in the chamber.

"Goddammit." Ben shot out of his chair, and out the door, slamming it closed behind him in disgust.

"What's his problem?" Turner asked.

I regarded Turner out of the corner of my eye.

"You really don't know?"

He held up two fingers, with his smoke between them.

"Scouts honor."

I shrugged. Dave was loading Ben's gun back up, and explained.

"Mr. Turner, after a cartridge is fired, the heat and pressure cause it to expand. This is both good, for the efficiency of the firearm, as it makes a gas tight seal on the back end, and bad for unloading the spent brass. That is why, as you can see," He held Ben's gun, barrel toward the table, out in front of him, with the cylinder open. "there's an ejector rod, that helps to press the tight fitting cartridges out of the chambers, for reloading." He pressed the ejector, making the .38 brass move up and down from the cylinder.

Turner got the picture, he was lighting a fresh smoke.

"So, you're saying that casing there was never fired? How'd they get the bullet out then?"

"With pliers, I believe. There is a small nick around the opening. Someone did bother to make an indentation in the primer, likely with whatever implement they used to remove the bullet, in an attempt to bolster their little charade."

Turner asked,

"What does all this mean, Trait?"

I guess we had really gotten to be good friends the night before, if he was asking me.

"Well, it could mean a few things. Who do you think might have put that in your pocket?"

He blew some more smoke. I could see a little now. He had let the act go completely when Dave was doing tricks with the pistol, but now I could just tell that the curtain had come back up. He had a poker face on that looked exactly like someone concerned should look.

"I don't know, John. Maybe Law? He's the only one, I'd think, that would have those kind of tools and know-how."

Dave opened his mouth to say something. He was still holding Ben's pistol, and looking hard at it. Before he got it out, the door opened and Ben popped his head in.

"You're free to go, Mr. Turner. We'll be in touch. No, we'll need to hold on to that jacket for a little while longer. Thank you."

Turner didn't need to be told twice. I didn't hold that against him either. The way it looked to me, Dave had helped him dodge a bullet by making the catch that there had been a non-explosive bullet removal. Turner could have sat in a cold Chicago cell for days, maybe even weeks, before someone had thought to make that catch. Let it be known also, that I'm not ruling Turner out either. There was still plenty of motive to go around. The next place I wanted to look was at Phillip Spencer. He had been friendly, giving me the dope on the troupe's romantic histories, but we didn't know anything about him. He had spent some time with Cindy Wilson, and now he was volunteering a discovery that made her current interest, Stanley Turner, the number one suspect. That seemed neat to me, and the neat ones usually don't make it past the first round of police questioning.

I sat there, thinking on that, rubbing my chin, for a moment. Ben Scott came back in, and sank back into his chair. Dave handed his pistol back to him, and he just dropped it down on the table with a thud. I could tell he was disappointed.

"I need to get back to the films." It was Dave, breaking the silence.

Ben and I offered a couple of yeps, and began gathering ourselves to go.

I was disappointed too. Dave had a plan of action, and short of a power outage, was likely to see it through without any hiccups. If I were him, I would go and buy a bunch of popcorn and some Cokes, and really make it fun. Meanwhile, Ben and I were up a stump. I had more people to track down, and likely spend the rest of my draw on, with no good idea of what I needed to find out from, or about, them. Ben's men had probably already let it slip up the grape vine, that they had found the much ballyhooed casing, and now Ben would have to tell the district attorney that it was a false alarm. Even though I was running around in cabs that I didn't have the personal funds for, a part of me was glad that I never had to make those kind of reports to a superior. I guess that's the sort of price you pay for financial security.

9

At the office I thought about calling Ralph back around to shuttle me to my three o'clock appointment at the scene of, the lawn art caper, that I needed to solve, but decided against it. I had planned on letting Ralph take me around for the day when I called him before, and he'd only gotten one measly fare out of it. I made some other calls, and answered one, before my watch said two, and it was time to get going. I headed down to the street and flagged down a cab. This fare would definitely be worth my driver's wile, as I was going all the way out to Elgin.

There was nothing to the job, and in the end I was glad that I had gone. The owners of the biggest house in a good neighborhood were missing a four foot tall concrete Venus de milo, that had sat on a pedestal, above a low hedge maze, in the back yard. Anybody could have made out the half dozen little footprints all around the base of the plinth. It was still cold, even around the expensive addresses. I paid a group of three kids two bucks each to let me in on the location of the stash from the heist, then another dollar to show me. Finally, under threat of turning them in for larceny, I parted with another two a piece, to make an even five, for them to lug it back from where it stood enshrined in their rouges hideout. The whole business took no more than an hour, and the homeowners were happy with my price of $150. Out on that side of society, on a Saturday, there were no cabs to hail, so I got to use the phone, and warm up inside my now previous client's pretty home.

I tell you all of that, though it has no bearing on our main story, just so you get the idea that Dave and I aren't always sitting around watching pictures, or wandering blindly around for dirt. Hell, sometimes we have to strictly type for our money too, but I've made those lamentations already. Before I left for Elgin, I'd called the seventh floor condo, and got Ally Lawrence. I wasn't looking for her, but took a moment for her anyway. She seemed to have forgiven me for conveying her from the scene of what must have surely been some sort of crime in the restaurant the night before. I told her she was a good dancer, and she said we should go again tonight. I accepted, as a strictly professional opportunity and obligation. I swear. With our second date set, and the wedding date pending, I got Fishman on the line.

He was who I had called for in the first place. He wanted badly to know why his star was being, as he put it, targeted. I didn't have much of an answer that I thought he'd like, so I just told him not to worry about it. I fished around and discovered that Stanley Turner had gone right back to the condo after our conference, and hadn't gone out again. The reason for my chat with Fishman was to figure out where this, Douglas Leech, and the rest of the company, should there be any, was put up. He said that Leech, and the rest of the nonessential help, was staying at a motel, on north edge of the south side, called the Washington. I got the address and let him know, to ease his mind about the money he was spending with us, that I would go and talk with them today. He liked that, told me to do all I could to help, and other such things that worried people do when you're trying to alleviate said worries, and I got off the phone.

It was five when I pulled up to the two story corner motel that had a name matching what he gave me. It was dark, but despite the light, I could tell that accommodations here, at the Washington, were nothing at all like the seventh floor condo. As the cab pulled away I stood with my hands in my pockets and looked through the glass of the shabby lobby. Across the street I saw a pool hall with a beer sign, and decided, if these extras were anything like the other Hollywood types, they surely weren't spending their furlough in their rooms reading paperbacks. I checked both ways for homicidal motorists, and hoofed it across the five lanes.

The pool hall was a combination dance hall, tavern, and restaurant. It could be that it doesn't take but one visit to, The Stiletto, or Williams', to spoil a man, but from where I took in the room, while handling my own coat, the dirty floor, hazy air, and faintly putrid smell of the place did not impress me. Aside from a couple of old men playing pool, the joint was deserted, save four jovial souls on barstools. One look, even at the back of them, said they were from out of town, and the fact that they only had one jacket between them, told me they had come from the warmer coast, and were just as far out of their meteorological comfort zone as the rest of the troupe. I walked up and sat down at the right of them. They greeted me. I introduced myself, and they did the same.

It was a diverse gathering, to say the least. There was Molly Fisher, obviously from New York, who was assistant to Cindy Wilson, in makeup. She was attractive, mid twenties, and blonde. She had the jacket. Next down from her was Mark Macin. He was a younger person also, that looked like he might as well star in something. He handled lighting. At his elbow, another kid, Matt Case, also lighting, but less star material. Finally, furthest down from me, was Douglas Leech. I got a surprise there, because Douglas Leech was a collection of unique things to the proceedings, so far. He was older, maybe thirty-five, English, right from London, and black. He, of course, was the clapper operator.

I ordered a beer, like the others had, and we grinned and chinned about the cold, and how Chicago is different from New York, and New York is different from L.A., and England is different from the U.S.. I was just glad that Leech wasn't working a movie in Atlanta, or maybe Dallas, or he might really had been dealing with some differences. Leech was the one I wanted to talk to the most. I didn't think the lighting crew, being a pair, and still not worthy of the five star treatment, would have too much insight into trips to Cuba or late night rendezvous. Leech however, from the rundown that Fishman had given Dave and I, seemed like an integral part of every scene, and even every take. If anybody might notice bullets and shells getting swapped around, my money was on him. I extracted him from the group on an invite for some pool, and we headed for the furthest table in a row of four.

It was turning out to be an outstanding weekend for my billiards. We racked up for nine ball this time, and I let Douglas break. He only caught a couple of chances to shoot in the first frame. During that first game, I tried to get the casual stuff out of the way. Discovering that he liked to be called Doug, that he had lived in California acting and working in pictures nearly his entire adult life, and that he only kept his west London accent on so thick because it surprised people to hear it. On the second game, he broke and made one, then missed right away. I made the one and two ball in order, and then got lucky on a combo, three-seven-nine in the corner, for the win.

"Mate, I think we need to find a snooker table." He said.

"You need to find another bar then, boy." That was one of the older gentlemen, that had been playing two tables down from us. I say, gentlemen, just as an example of my own decency and manners. The two of them had come around to the end of the next table closest to us, by the wall. The talker leaned on his stick, and said some more.

"Why don't you take your snooker, and your cockney talk, back to where you came from?"

Doug took them in out of the corner of his eye, with his chin up.

"I'm from California, mate. I didn't know you all had some problem with other types of pool tables in these parts." He shot them a pearly white grin.

My personal policy on disliking people by default is based on a lot of things. Whether they like nine ball, eight ball, or snooker is certainly not in the running. Whether a guy's black isn't either, which was certainly these guy's problem. I had my prejudices, like anybody else, until I got off in France, and the cook for our unit, Clint Carter, a black man, single handedly took out six Germans who had snuck into our camp, and were prepared to mow us down. I'll tell you more about Clint another time, but the short version is that we were all in a bad way, and a lot of men came to think a lot better of Clint, and his kind, that day. Clint lived in the city, and Dave and I used him for things now. He had enlightened me years ago, and so if the opportunity presented itself, like this, then I liked to pass it on.

The man talking looked to be around fifty, but maybe closer to sixty. He had a grey beard with tobacco stains around his mouth. He looked tired. His playing partner, and likely career follower, didn't cut any better figure. Their interjection, which I decided I would disparage immediately, did present an opportunity however, to endear myself to Doug, and maybe make my conversational interrogation even easier.

The leader put a finger in Doug's chest, and tried to sound mean. "I want you out of here." He tacked on a word that he meant to be a pejorative, but I don't feel like it's worth the letters.

Doug calmly took the old man by his wrist, and pushed the hand back toward its owner. As you might imagine, that was enough to justify what they had come over to do.

We all four were holding cues, but in an obvious tell that this was largely a recreational conflict, the leader sat his down on our table. His friend did likewise, so Doug and I obliged as well. I was already starting to like Doug.

The old man that had been talking, fired an uppercut toward Doug. It didn't have any legs in it though, and Doug blocked it with his forearm, and put his shoulder into him, pushing him into the wall. I thought that was a good time to get involved, and so took a step forward, and socked his partner in the side of the neck under his jaw. Pushing off the wall, the first man made a run at Doug. Doug stepped to the side, got low, and came up with an uppercut of his own, into his middle. It was a good shot too, and stopped the old man in his tracks. He stayed doubled over, and went to his knees. My man had gone for a near aerial assault, with a high looping right hand. I went ahead and took it on the top of the head. I'd left my hat on the rack at the door, so there was no danger. He was wide open. I punched him in his belly, putting some good hip action into the shot, and he went down also.

"I think you two are gonna have to go ahead and cash out of this business on the ground floor." A bit wordy, I know, but I was excited.

They got the message and made it to their feet. The bartender had just watched, and now called them by name, seconding my motion. On the way out the door they intimated that I might be romantically involved in the affairs of the minorities. In so many words. So I told them that if they wanted to continue discussing it, I'd be stamping my official statements with right hands. In so many words. The leader waved me off, and left with his friend in tow.

"We had your back, Doug!" That was Molly, from her barstool. Doug's compatriots had swiveled around, and by the way they laughed, and by the way a dollar changed hands between the two lighting boys, had enjoyed the show.

Doug laughed and made a gesture at them. He turned to me, and asked, "So mate, what do you want to know?"

We continued our talk a few doors down, at a

cafe. It was almost six, and I hadn't eaten since I left my house that morning. The excitement at the pool hall had me ravenous. We ordered some burgers and fries. Cheese included. The staff knew Doug from the past weeks, so we likely wouldn't be interrupted again.

"So, Doug, what can you tell me about the other night, with Roker? What take were you on, things like that."

Doug thought for a minute, and answered.

"We were on the third take when you walked out. All it was, was Steve running into the shot, down the sidewalk, with Stanley behind. Then Steve was supposed to turn around and say, "I'm not going any further, Smith.". That had messed us up on the first take, because he had started saying the line before he had turned, and the sound wasn't any good that way.

"Take two was better. He stopped, got turned around, said the line, and then he was supposed to draw his pistol."

"What happened with his pistol?"

"He didn't have it. It was supposed to be in the breast pocket of his overcoat. It was so cold that night that everything had been staged in the costume trailer, but Law had been late coming from the condo and must have missed it."

The burgers had come, so we were eating and talking between bites now. I put in,

"So you all had been on a break before that?"

Doug swallowed, and continued.

"Yeah, we had shot some of the chase outside, earlier in the evening. The director had noticed, late the night before, how at a certain hour the steam would start to rise up from the drains. He thought it would look better that way, so we'd gone back to the flat to wait, and warm up."

"I see. So then Law outfitted everyone with their guns?"

"Not quite. Even though Steve didn't have his gun, once we cut, Fishman said to go ahead and play it out. So Steve drew a finger gun, and Stanley had his. He fired the first shot, Steve fell down, and then Stanley took a couple steps forward, and fired another to finish him off. Steve did a little jump. It looked good."

I was impressed by Doug's recall, and asked,

"I don't know much about making these pictures, but you seem to be important to the operation. Why do they house you out here with the lighting crew?"

He dropped his shoulders a bit, and gave me a look that said something along the line of, "Do you have to ask?", but he explained anyway.

"It was Roker. Ally and Stanley, everyone else up there really, were all for me staying in the condo, and with them on the other films too. They're good people. Roker wouldn't have it though. Said it could,

"Hurt his brand.". He was the main star of the company, even though he was just the baddie in this one, so they had to let him have his way."

Not that anybody ever deserves to die, and certainly not when they're working and not on their own time, but since people are cut down in all kinds of ways every day, I was beginning to be of the opinion that Steve Roker had deserved what he got as much as anybody. He had been reported, so far, to be a womanizer, a drug distributor, and a racist. Those don't strike me as traits conducive to anyone's good brand.

Back around to the shooting though.

"Well, tell me about the third take."

"Alright. I saw Law come out with his pouch. I turned around and started erasing and rewriting the clapper. I think Law went to Roker first, but I'm not sure. There was a little snag with the camera, but only for a second. We'd been having a time with it, because of the cold. Once that got settled, I stepped in and called it off, and we started. It went like it was supposed to, until you came out of the theatre. That doorway was right in the top right hand corner of the shot, and the light was on you as well. Sometimes we can keep an unintended extra walking through, but not on an important scene like that."

"How far into it were you before I spoiled it?"

"Steve had just said his line and drawn his gun.

Turner fired right as you walked out."

"He fired that second shot after I heard some-body yell cut. Why did he do that?"

Doug motioned that he didn't know, and said so.

"I don't know, mate. You'd have to ask him. He might not have heard it, with the echo coming through the alley, or he might have been locked in on the scene. Anyway, Roker had fallen down, like last time, but I didn't see what happened after that, exactly, because I was looking at you. Once I saw we'd missed it, I started filling out the next board."

"So you never saw anybody messing with Turner's gun?"

"Just Law. Like always. Hey, are you coming to that blues club tonight?"

That was a wide swing in subject. I didn't have much else to try to get out of him anyway, so I followed along.

"Blues Club? Ally Lawrence invited me dancing tonight. Is that where she plans to go?"

He had finished his food, and wiped his mouth with the napkin.

"Yes, she called Molly too, to make sure we were all coming along. The Blues House, at nine. She's send-ing a car for all of us. She said for us all to wear blue, but I'll have to see what I have washed."

We talked a little more about odds and ends. I

paid the tab. Doug had insisted he leave the tip, but I got that too, and told him that he had ate on his boss's dime anyway. With the blues house, this evening, it would really make a good sampling of Chicago night life for me this weekend. As someone usually without enough dough for public revelry, it was certainly a change of pace. I needed a change of clothes too. A bit of ketchup had found my shirt, and the jacket I was wearing was grey. I had an hour to get back to my apartment and get ready. I wondered too, who would attend. I needed to talk to Phillip Spencer, about just what made him think to check Stanley Turner's coat pocket. Also, with the nickel plated .32 still in my pocket, I thought I needed to talk to Law about the last time it had been used in a scene, and what had made Ally Lawrence think she had been walking around with the prop gun. Detective Scott had no doubt asked her that already, but I felt like she and I had a bit of an understanding. Scott hadn't danced with her, after all.

10

At the apartment I got a shave and a shower double quick. In going along with the theme, I dug out what I call my Dave jacket. A dark navy thing with just two buttons. I also called Dave at his house but didn't get him. Hopefully he had decided something warranted looking into, but then he could have been too enthralled in his new film collection to get to the phone. Maybe still, he might have rearranged his place again, leaving the phone entirely inaccessible. It wasn't that bad a loss not to have him along though. Dave doesn't like films much, but he regards parties, and that sort of get together, with a visible disdain. That's to say nothing of his opinion of any music produced in the last two hundred years. I, on the other hand, feel similarly about most compositions meant for the harpsichord.

A cab dropped me off at the spot just five minutes after nine, and I went in. It was a good sized room, purpose built for shows like this one. There was a five piece band, with an organ and a sax player. They were just starting as I entered, and a man that I suspected would sing, was letting the crowd know what they were in for, with a musical backdrop to his monologuing. I surrendered my overcoat at the door, and stood listening and surveying the crowd. It was a good mix of folks. Doug would have a good few of his clan for a change. I liked that. They also had no problem breaking the ice on the dance floor, so it looked like it would be a good night for everyone. To the left was a stairway that led up to a second floor balcony that overlooked the stage below. A bar was along the whole right wall, with people leaning with their backs to it, to see the band. The dance floor was nearly as large as the one at Stiletto had been. No chandelier, but colored lights instead.

"Hello, again, Mr. Trait." It was Molly Fisher, and the rest of the motel crew. I said hello, and we all shook hands.

Doug said, "Ally reserved us a table upstairs. Come on."

We all followed Doug up to a long table with a reserved sign in the middle. It was close to the railing of the overlook. I took a seat on the corner, with my back to the band, so I would be able to see everyone at the table, and down on the dance floor, with just a small adjustment. For the next twenty minutes the motel crew and I cut up about mine and Doug's altercation, from earlier, and had a round of drinks. Finally, some of the stars began to trickle in. Fashionably late, I suppose.

The first ones in were Stanley Turner, wearing a

sharp blue suit. He had Cindy Wilson on his arm, who had her makeup hand on display, with blue smoky eyes. It was a bit much for my taste, but it certainly made an impression. Bringing up the rear, and seeming to have the idea to turn that little sub-group into a tricycle, was Phillip Spencer. For being in charge of the costume trailer, he didn't seem to wear his talents like the rest of them. He had come in black slacks, and a medium blue button up. That was it. They sat down and ordered drinks. Molly and Cindy complimented one another's makeup, and then talked about what I guess they would call work. The talk of shadows and rouge was all lost on me. Stanley smoked, as usual, gulped at a scotch, and appeared impatient. My guess being that he was mostly here for Ally Lawrence. Another twenty minutes would pass before she made her entrance.

When Ally finally did arrive, it came with a little fanfare. The band finished a song, and I looked down at them and gave them a hand. Looking down, I spied Walter Fishman in front of the stage. He was talking to the singer-guitar player. The band leader straightened up from the conference, and announced on the mic for us all to put our hands together and welcome Hollywood actress Ally Lawrence. People did as they were told. Ally came in, and appeared in my view at the middle of the dance floor. She was wearing a form fitting red dress, and little black hat with a small lace veil. She raised her arms over her head with a flourish, turned on the spot, and finished with a little bow to the adoring public. I would have clapped for her even if she hadn't been a movie star. She looked stunning. With that through, she joined Fishman, who waited for her off to the side of the dance floor, and let him have her elbow as they ascended the stairs. Everyone at the table greeted her with more enthusiasm than I ever felt comfortable with displaying. Then again, I can't see myself on a movie set trying to pretend I'm a shoeshine boy, or maybe a POW. I'm no shut in, by any means, but it takes a different breed for show business.

Overall it was a good time. The band was loud, as blues bands tend to be, so I did my best to read lips. Even the conversations I was meant to be a part of involved a good deal of shouting. On the other side of the upstairs there was a doorway where you could go out to an outdoor balcony on the front of the building, to get some air. I got Doug's attention and got him outside. There was a cold breeze blowing, so we talked fast.

"Doug, I thought of something else I meant to ask you earlier." He just said, "Shoot.", and rubbed his arms. "Ok. When was the last time a scene had called for Ally to use that silver .32?"

He closed his eyes tight, and thought hard for a moment.

"It was Thursday."

"The day of the shooting?"

"Yeah, it was a little before lunch. We had a scene where Ally was supposed to shoot at Stanley. Her character was like a sidekick to Steve's big baddie. I think we tried a dozen takes. Steve was stuck on a line about how, "It was time for you to go, Mr. Smith.", and then he was supposed to say some things about how Ally couldn't shoot, but he couldn't get the timing right. The scene called for Ally to fire three, four, maybe even five times, and Rob said he was nearly out of blanks for her gun, so we decided to come back to it after lunch, or the next day."

"Alright, and then when you all got done, Law took the guns back up?"

Doug showed me his palms.

"You'd have to ask him about that, mate. He always does, but I didn't see."

"It's alright, pal. You've been a big help. Let's get back inside before we freeze to death."

I held the door, and let Doug through, then hurried in myself. I got back to my chair and tried to get an eye on everyone again. It was just myself, Doug, one of the lighting boys, and Stanley Turner at the table. The lighting boy, Matt, said that the girls had gone down to the bar. That was mostly true. I spotting Ally and Fishman dancing close down below to a slow blues song. Stanley Turner was turned in his chair, and staring at them. He got up abruptly, shot his hand into his breast pocket for his pack, and headed down the stairs. I wondered if there was about to be a bout, and debated with myself on whether to hurry down so I could intervene, or if I should stay where I was, as it was the best seat in the house for taking in the headline card. Turner must have slowed a little as he made his approach. He came in casually enough, save for a little incidental contact with Fishman, who was making a turn, and asked to cut in. His request was received gentlemanly enough, and Fishman stepped off. Blues bands play good long songs. Too long, if you don't care for dancing, but Ally and Turner didn't seem to mind. They danced extra close, and it wouldn't have surprised me, if at any moment, Cindy Wilson had come up and broken up the proceedings. She and Ally would have certainly drawn good numbers for their rematch, but it didn't happen.

Fishman had gone straight for the stairs. In no big hurry, he arrived back at the table. He gave me a nod, and took a seat at the other end. Not long after he made it back, the rest of the crew returned with a tray of shots and drinks. Molly asked where Ally was, and someone said dancing. Cindy hollered over the railing, down to Ally, that she had a drink for her. I glanced around at some of the other patrons, who were mostly content, but some seemed to say with their faces, that my group was a little much. Turner came back up without Ally, saying she told him that she had to freshen up. That was a ten minute wait, but Ally finally arrived. If you didn't know to look, you probably wouldn't have noticed the subtle head change, but it was there. I of course didn't show that

I had paid any mind, but Stanley Turner looked furious. Or at least he looked like someone who was trying to act not furious, while being furious. Since our meeting with him at the police station, I was beginning to feel like I had a bit of a line on what he showed and didn't show. This time it was the larger gulps of scotch, and the more aggressive flicks of his cigarette ashes, that betrayed him. They didn't fit with the charming smile that he had affixed to himself.

If you're keeping a head count, like I was, then you've probably noticed that I haven't mentioned any interactions, or observations, concerning the young Rob Law, who seemed to have such an important part to play in all of this. I decided to find out about it, and got an opportunity to follow Fishman down to the bar, and ordered next to him. I asked if Rob was coming.

"I don't know, Mr. Trait. I figured he'd be here by now. Sometimes he runs late."

"I've heard he was late Thursday night, and that's why Roker didn't have his prop for the first take. Any idea what he was doing?"

Fishman shrugged. His tone told me, right off, that he had something on his mind that he wanted to tell me. I put eyes on him that said, you can tell me anything, old buddy, and he must have decided he could.

"I think I need to level with you about something, Mr. Trait, but first I need to know. Are you and Mr. DeGrabber under any obligation to report everything to the Police directly? I mean, I know you would have to report a serious crime that hurt someone, but what about, inconsistencies?"

I took a deep breath, and put on my sincere face.

"Listen, Mr. Fishman. We work for you. While we have a reasonable obligation, as citizens, to report things like murders, if you've got something that you felt like needed to sound one way, and now might sound another, we won't hold that kind of thing against you. It may turn out not to have anything to do with the case anyway, and then the cops certainly won't need to know. You see?"

That seemed to ease his mind. He motioned me over to a small table, and we sat down with our drinks. I was buzzing about whatever he might tell me, so I put my drink to my lips so they wouldn't let him know I was smiling inside.

He began. "The other day, when the Police found that $500 dollars in Robert's closet. The truth is, I do think he got it from me." He lowered his voice, and leaned a little closer. "I don't know if you've found out, but Ally developed a type of habit while we were filming one of my pictures in Florida. I'm not the partying type really, but I'm not so decrepit as to not see what I have with her. I however, don't maintain any contacts of the sort she requires. Anyway, I have been paying Robert to, uhm… assist me in getting the things that Ally wants, that I can't just pick up for her on Rodeo Drive. I think he's been skimming me, and that's how he came to have that money put away."

I nodded my head, and stayed somber.

"So has Law missed any of these deliveries lately?"

"No, he's come through every time, but I don't really know what I'm buying exactly. I told the police that he must have saved it, and I found out from him, that he said it had been a bonus from me. I just don't want to get caught in something that could further jeopardize my work, or Ally's career. That was the whole point of using Robert. He is very discrete and detail oriented. You see? But he's also a bit greedy."

I told him I understood, and got to my feet.

"Is Rob running one of these errands tonight?"

"He went earlier today." He looked up at me, over his thin glasses, and seemed ashamed.

I nodded. "Come on, director. We don't want to miss the party."

Agreeing with that, we made our way back up to the gathering.

From that point on, as Saturday slipped into Sunday, the band got louder, and the jokes between songs got funnier. The Hollywood bunch took over the joint. Girls were attracted to our group by Turner and the better looking of the two lighting boys, and also by Ally. She was a picture of what they wanted to be. People wanted to be close to that. Next thing I knew, our table upstairs was largely just a place to hold drinks and glasses. The chairs were full and strangers stood all around. I had kept my post at the corner of the table, but had added a red head, named Jennifer, to my lap. DeGrabber and I keep the office closed, usually, on Sundays, so my excuse is that I was off the clock. Everybody had a turn dancing with every one else. Ally pulled me away a few times to the dance floor. The second or third time down, I thought to look up, and saw I was under the watchful gaze of Fishman and Turner.

Doug decided to have fun with playing a plantation waiter. He told me he did a lot of parts in pictures in that kind of role. He did an incredible southern accent too. It seemed like he was continually running trays of shots from the bar. Each time up he'd say something silly with the accent on, and take a shot himself. After a half dozen or so trips, the accent started to slip, but that just made it funnier. I was handling my share of the shot tray too. Around two thirty the band announced it was time for their last number. Everyone took their partner and headed down for a last dance. By that time us men were spoiled for choice of partner, but I stuck to the one I'd sat with. As I got up to go dance, I found my legs had decided to change lengths on me. The spinning on the dance floor was doing my head in. When the song finally ended, and it was time to go, I guess I didn't look quite myself.

"You gonna make it, mate? You can ride back with us. Ally's invited everyone back to the flat." It was Doug. He seemed to be holding up pretty well. Maybe he'd burned some off with all the trips up and down.

I just mumbled that that sounded swell to me. I remember reaching for some money, and someone telling me they had it. I think Fishman footed the bill. I shudder to think what it must have been. These weren't the gaudy prices of lakeshore drive, but the quantity of the order had been prodigious. The standing and walking around, was doing nothing more for my head than the dancing had. I vaguely recall getting my coat and hat on, with some help from what's her name, and getting put in a really long looking taxi cab. It seemed like someone put a long stemmed glass in my hand while I was in there, but maybe it was a cigarette. The next day, or in about five minutes, I couldn't tell which, we arrived outside the building. I had a fleeting thought, as Doug and I passed by Williams', that I needed to ask them something, but couldn't remember what. I also thought, at the same time, that Doug seemed to have his face very close to mine, then realized that I was not mobile strictly on my own say so. He was holding me up. He finally got me to the elevator and leaned me against the wall. The cold night air on the way in, seemed to be rejuvenating me, and I started to become aware of just how sloppy I was. That was embarrassing, but no one seemed to mind.

After a good long lean, the elevator stopped, and we piled out and into the condo. I worked my way over to a big couch, and flopped down in the corner of it. Jennifer, from the club, had apparently got the invite too, and came and joined me there. She put my arm around her, and then I think I dozed off. It was a loud and busy sounding place, as I half laid there. Once my head was back the room seemed to pirouette, so I decided I'd better not try to look. It wasn't long before I was brought to my senses. From somewhere in front of me, across the main room, I heard a scream that sounded familiar. There was also the sound of breaking glass. My mind told the rest of me to get up and look into it, but the rest of me decided it was probably a false alarm. Another scream, this time closer.

Time to get up. My eye's popped open. I shoved my blanket off. She had been asleep too, and jumped to her feet. I was on mine, looking straight at Ally Lawrence. She was standing in a doorway, that I figured led off to some of the bedrooms, with her hands down at her sides screaming. People rushed to her. As they approached she motioned back through the opening. Saying, "In there. In there. It's terrible.", and other nonspecific unhelpful things like that. I started toward her and followed the few that had gone through. I went through a bedroom, and into a large bathroom. Some glass crunched under my shoe soles as I stepped in.

It was a big tile job. Slate grey on the floor and

the walls, in big two foot squares. There was a double sink, a tub big enough for three, and a walk in shower, all glass, with two shower heads. There were a couple of small rugs where you would step out of the shower and bath, and where you would stand to brush your teeth, so you wouldn't slip and break a hip. Rob Law lay in the middle of the floor, in front of the sinks, with slipping being the least of his worries. You could say Rob Law was worry free now. One look at his pale blueish visage was all anyone needed to see he was dead, and had been for some time. The large knife that protruded from his chest, on the left side, just below his rib cage, was a tell also.

I've read, that just because something makes you feel like it, that you don't actually sober up. It's strictly a matter of time and chemistry. If that's true, then maybe it's just that some things can happen that make you try harder to see through the fog. The sight of young Rob Law, there dead on the ground, motivated me to maximum effort. A look around at the faces of my new friends showed me a couple of things. First, they were in no better condition than I was. And second, that they were falling into panic, and needed someone to take charge.

I shouted to get their attention. All the voices raised to drown me out. The entire condo was in the bathroom, some around the body, and others pushing into the back of me, as I stood in the threshold. I heard some assertion that we had to hide the body, and even some people's agreement. It was getting out of hand fast. I tried a few more times to yell for order. Fishman was by the body, and started to reach down for the knife. That kind of tampering wouldn't do at all. I dove into my jacket pocket and pulled out Ally Lawrence's .32. I hadn't found the midst of a night out to be a good time to rearm her, and still had it handy. I aimed for the corner, where the floor tile met and wall tile, and fired a shot. It was so loud. The shot skipped off the floor, and into the wall. It hit the ceiling, and brought a bit of plaster dust down, but didn't have enough to do any real harm after its deflections. Some guests behind me retreated back at least to the bedroom. The ones in front froze.

"Don't touch anything." I commanded. "Doug. Doug! Where's Doug?" Doug came up behind me.

"I'm here."

"Doug, watch this door, and don't touch anything. The rest of you, out. We have to call the police. Now! Send the rest of the company home."

Fishman stood up and looked like he wanted to make a protest, but decided against it, and went out. I left Doug at the door, and went for a phone. There was one by the bed, right behind me. I got on it and dialed a number.

"Hello."

"Dave, it's John."

"John, I'm glad you've called. I've just been viewing a film called, "The Deft Touch". It's a film staring

Stanley Turner, from before his time with Mr. Fish-"

"Dammit, Dave. I don't have time for a film review right now. I'm here at Fishman's condo, and Rob Law is dead, in a bathroom, with a knife in his chest. I'm doing my best, but I'm not in much good condition right now."

"Was it Phillip Spencer?"

"Dave, I don't have any idea. He was with us when we went out tonight."

"Mr. Law was Stanley Turner's best way to get out of this." Dave sounded like he was thinking out loud. It made me a little sore that he was being so nonchalant at a time like this.

"Dave, I don't have time to speculate right now. Are you coming up here? I'm gonna be caught up in the questioning. Maybe if you make it here before the police, you can work on the tenants."

"I need a report from you. Can you get away?"

I shrugged, and rubbed my head to try to clear some more fog.

"I probably can, but they may arrest me tomorrow."

"They can find you at the office then. Come to me."

I told him I would, and hung up. I took another hard look at the bathroom to get the picture, patted Doug on the shoulder, and took off.

On the way out, I tried to take more pictures of all the faces as I saw them. They were all around the little corner bar, trying to get their constitutions fortified, and comforting Ally. She was on a stool crying into a handkerchief. Stanley Turner had a cigarette hanging from his lip, looking grim. He had his arm around Cindy Wilson. She was doing the same as Ally. The motel crew, minus Doug, were around and behind the bar, drinking from various bottles, and looking a reasonable mix of scared and concerned. Fishman was right by Ally. He looked sick. By the door, at a phone, I passed by Phillip Spencer. He was telling the police that they had discovered a body on the premises. He didn't look, or sound, overly concerned. I put it in the file.

Outside the condo door, I made a right down the hallway. I was looking for a service elevator, or even a stairwell. I found some stairs, and nearly jumped down from landing to landing. I didn't want to be met by the city officials while I fled the scene. At ground level a door let me out into the cold again. This time, the excitement and the air, did sober me up. Science be damned. I hurried around the corner, up an alleyway, right down another, and came out on the street opposite the entrance to the condo. I stayed on foot for another two blocks, then hailed a cab. I gave the driver Dave's address, and made my escape, with the noise of faint sirens in the distance behind me.

On the way to Dave's I checked my watch. 4:00 am. I had been asleep for a little while on the couch, and there was no getting a report of that time out of my bean. I got my thoughts arranged, the best I could, about the night. Chiefly, about the order that everyone had shown up in. There wasn't much to it. Myself first. Then the motel crew. Cindy, Stanley, and Phillip, then Ally and Fishman. Had Fishman killed his supplier for skimming money off of him? If he had, then why did he pick the very night, right after bumping him off, to tell me that he had had nefarious dealings with him anyway? I thought a bit about Dave's comment, on the phone, about Law being Turner's way out. I guess that was true, if we could ever find that Law had had that .38 casing. That put me onto a thought, that maybe whoever had planted that bogus brass in Turner's pocket, might be meaning to make Turner for it by any means necessary. So much for straightening out what happened tonight. I decided I would just have to tell the story slow, and work out the kinks as I came to them. The taxi pulled up to Dave's building. I got out and headed up.

11

At Dave's I repeated the whole rigmarole of passing my overcoat through the crack and sidling through. His place was still laid out like the Chinese Theater. Dave, and his apartment, looked unkept to say the least. It was dark, save for a lamp in the bedroom that scarcely illuminated anything when the projector was off. As I stepped in my feet disturbed a collection of some two dozen pop cans that had been piled at the corner of the couch. Dave hadn't bothered to get up. He'd only reached back from his seat on the couch and released the door latch. He was wearing his usual dark blue jacket and black shoes. The shoes needed polishing, and the jacket looked like it would need a press. There was no telling when either would get the attention they needed. Dave's face was unshaven, and he had bags under his eyes. I moved some film canisters off the couch, and sank down into it.

Dave wanted everything from the last time I'd seen him, onto now. I was excited. I didn't know if the police might send someone after me, and wanted to tell him about the latest developments first, but he insisted he would have to have the earlier dope before he'd be able to do anything.

I gave it to him in full. I breezed through my trip to Elgin, and he made no interjections about it. He wanted, and got, descriptions of the entire motel crew. He got especially down to the tacks about what Doug had to say about the scenes and takes. I gave him our evening in full, as best as I could remember it. He wanted to know the order that people danced in. Did anyone get left out. How many times did Ally dance with who. I closed my eyes and tried to picture it as I had seen it from my overlook. I was able to put it together with a good degree of certainty, until around 12:30. At the inclusion of my second conference with Doug, he took interest in Thursday's earlier film shoot, where Roker had botched it. It was his opinion, from seeing Roker's performances on screen, that something must have been going on at that time, already. He wanted to know my opinion of Douglas Leech, and I told him I rated him highly. Now we got to the parts that I was fuzzy on. I could tell Dave was bothered by my loosing track, but he didn't show it so much with his attitude. He did, however ask me some six different ways, how it was that I let myself get over served. Seeing that I was, even now, indefensibly drunk, he wanted to know the travails of the drinks tray, in full, also. I tried to humor him, but the only answer I had for it all, was that it had been a good time, and that was the truth. He didn't understand that, because David DeGrabber, I don't think, has good times. He decided he had to accept it.

"So you were asleep on the couch. How long?"

"At the time, I didn't know. Looking back, about an hour and a half."

"You say Law was long dead?"

"That's right. The blood had dried around him. I figure somebody off'd him before anyone left for the Blues House. The motel crew didn't have time, Ally Lawrence has no motive really, and Fishman would have to have been a fool to kill him right before he was the last man out."

"Where did the knife come from?"

I shook my head.

"No telling. Looked like a large kitchen knife, to me. I didn't stick around to check any of that."

The bag looked empty and Dave knew it. He stood up.

"We'll have to find out what happened tomorrow. I'll call Detective Scott in the morning, and see if he'll save us some leg work, if we'll turn you in to him without resistance."

"Oh, thanks a lot."

He waved it off.

"You weren't there before or during the slaying. He shouldn't actually need you anymore than he needs any of the strangers from the club. He likely will only want you on principal alone."

I got up to head out. Principal alone, sounded harmless enough, but it would still likely cause a headache in the morning. On principal alone, they might get me down to the station, and decide to pay back some for my sticking my nose into things. I thought to ask Dave what he had found in his film study, but decided my bed sounded more appealing. Especially if I were to spend the next night in the can. He held the door open the crack, and handed my coat through to the hallway. I had to walk a few blocks, before a night cab cruised past. I got in, and was back home in no time. The sky was already getting a hint of blue outside my window, so I skipped my nightly rituals, and went straight for the hay.

A few hours later, the alarm sounded my awakening. My head pounded, and my teeth had donned a sweater around them. A shower, shave, and a brush, had me back looking presentable, and feeling like I might persist, as long as I wasn't asked to attend any more dances anytime soon. I made my way downstairs, and caught a cab to the office.

Sid, our doorman, was behind his desk with a half box of doughnuts, working on his figure over a morning paper. He addressed me like normal, but it seemed loud to me this morning.

"Good morning, John. Did you see another one of those actors got murdered last night?"

"I was there, Sid. They got any pictures?"

"Just one of the dame. Says here council's probably not gonna renew their permits. That's a shame, huh? Not having a movie made right here in Chicago. I wanted to see it."

"If they can't keep the troupe upright, they can't finish it anyway." I told him, as I got in the elevator and pushed the button.

When I arrived in the hallway the office door was standing open, and a welcome party was within. Dave was at his desk. He looked as though he had opted to forego his rituals this morning. His usual unkept hair, was now accompanied by spotty whiskers. Ben Scott was sat in my desk chair, and he had his shoes up on my desk, which didn't thrill me. Compared to Dave and I, he looked like a picture of rest and prideful appearance. He had on some black wing tips, freshly shined. You'd have thought they were new, if the soles hadn't been visible; showing signs of mileage. He had on his long grey coat and matching hat. A cigarette burned under his red mustache. Along the wall, to my left in the row of clients chairs, sat one of Scott's uniformed men. Next to him, sat a cold, tired, dejected looking, Walter Fishman.

Scott addressed me energetically.

"Good morning, Trait. We've just been talking about you. Fishman was going over again how you fired a shot in a closed space in a public building, ran everyone out of the room, and then beat the street yourself. I was surprised this morning, when DeGrabber told me I could find you here today, and now I'm shocked you showed. I'm glad you saved me the APB."

I thought maybe he was putting me on. He looked too happy. It could have just been the state of my head, making anyone in proper frame of mind appear downright joyous by comparison. I didn't want to push any luck I might get, so I pulled around one of the client chairs, and set it at the end of my desk, like we have the suspects do.

"Ben, you know I wouldn't just run out on you and stay gone. How would we ever catch the bad guy working like that?" I shot him a grin. He had a grin on, but now wiped it off, and started in on me.

"Listen, Trait. I wasn't the first person DeGrabber got on the horn with this morning. Fishman here, called me, and said that, since you both are his representation in this thing, that he wanted you two to be around for his questioning, and other contacts. When he realized you had skipped last night, he clammed up tight. Now, we tried to break him loose, but he wouldn't budge until DeGrabber talked to him this morning. I know you two ultimately are on my side on this, and don't want a murderer running around any more than I do, so since I was duty bound to find you anyway, Trait, I figured we could all get together for a little powwow."

That all struck me as sounding like some kind of Christmas present. No box, no hot light, no chair with two short legs. They might not even make me draw anything on the A room blackboard to incriminate myself with. Sign me up. It was just a testament to the affects a good nights sleep can have, even on a police man. I told Scott to ask me anything. He started with me on the couch, asleep. We got to the part where I called Dave, and left, and that was the bag. I said, that for anything more, I'd need to hear what had happened before anyone left for The Blues House. Scott tried to skate on us, but Fishman reiterated that he would only discuss things in our presence, so he brought his chair around next to me, in front of Dave's desk, and started.

"Turner came back around four. He said he had walked from the police station, and stopped at a shop for a carton of smokes."

I put in.

"Detective Scott, since I'm still working for the director, do you mind if I take notes?" Scott grunted and moved out of the way so I could fish a notebook and pen out of my desk. Now equipped, I settled in for the story.

"So, like I was saying. Turner got in at four, and we hung around a while, until the car arrived for us at nine, and left."

Scott shook his head in disapproval.

"Keep thinking, director. We questioned everybody at the condo last night. Let's not miss the details. What did Turner do when he got in yesterday?"

Fishman sank a little in his seat, sighed deep, and

found a good bit more to tell.

"Turner came in like a freight train. He busted through the door. Ally and I were on the couch, and the way he hit it, I thought it was a break in. He sat two cartons of cigarettes down by the sink, and went straight for Phillip's room."

Dave, "Where's Mr. Spencer's room?"

"It's across the main room. Opposite where Robert's was. There are two that way. Cindy Wilson's is back there also."

"Continue."

"Well, it didn't take one of you sleuths to tell that, by the look on his face, he meant to do somebody harm. There were voices raised as soon as he got back to the hallway. We heard a thud. That's when we decided to go see what it was about. Ally and I got to our feet and started that way, but before we made it to the hall, Phillip rushed out into the main room with Stanley on his heels. He was saying that he didn't know what Stanley was talking about. Stanley was saying something about trying to get him killed."

Scott got in.

"Did you ask Mr. Turner what it was about? Did he tell you?"

"Yes. He told all of us."

"Who all was present at the time?" That was Dave again.

Fishman thought for a moment.

"It was myself, Ally, Stanley, and Phillip, in the main room. Cindy came out of her room, only after the shouting had really kicked up. I demanded what it was all about, and Stanley said Phillip had planted phony evidence that he had killed Steve, and tried to give it to the police. He was shoving Phillip around as he told us. He kept screaming at Phillip to admit it, and he did."

Scott, as cops do, seemed to take that personally.

"He admitted to trying to jam him up?"

Fishman scratched nervously at his face.

"Not right off. Stanley was roughing him up. Ally had a hold of his coat tail, but he's not a small man. He kept pushing Phillip around the room, into things, and knocking stuff over, until he knocked him over a coffee table and broke it. There on the floor, was when Phillip came off it. He said, "Yeah, I put it there. You took Cindy from me. You shot Steve anyway. There's no denying that. You should pay as much as anyone else." Then Stanley spat in his face, and started for the door. He left. I don't know where he went."

Dave said, "Did Mr. Turner do anything else before he left? Anything at all?"

Fishman tilted his head and answered.

"What? Like grab a knife from the kitchen and go and stab Robert to death?"

Scott had lost most of his good humor.

"No need for sarcasm, Mr. Fishman. Where was Robert Law while all of this was going on?"

The director looked around a bit. He made fists and released them a couple of times to make sure his hands still worked. I had to resist an urge to give him a signal with my face, to go ahead and spill what Rob Law had probably been out doing, but Scott had us both in plain view. Fishman needed that signal too. He seemed determined to make things hard for himself. He simply said,

"Rob was out."

Scott leaned forward, in my chair, and regarded Fishman's darting eyes and dejected posture. He stared at him and lit another smoke without taking his eyes off him. After a few seconds, he blew smoke, and said,

"Out, huh? He was just out." He raised his voice a good deal. "When did he get back?"

Fishman had gone head shy now. Pulling back from the words like they threatened to slap his face. He stammered some giving his answer.

"Stanley patted his pockets on the way to the door, and went back to the table. He grabbed a whole carton of smokes, and rushed back toward the door. When he flung it open, Rob was standing there with his key in his hand."

Scott gave a little half smile, and leaned back in

my chair again.

"Good. See, Mr. Fishman. That wasn't so hard to get through, now that we're through. Let's see if we can't keep this running smoothly. No more speed bumps. Yeah?"

Fishman nodded.

"Describe Mr. Law, as you saw him in the door, upon his return." That was Dave. He had his chair turned, feet out in front of him, and his hands together in front of his mouth. No notes necessary.

"You mean, like what was he wearing?" Everything out of the director was steeped in worry now. He looked from Dave to Scott. Dave nodded, and Fishman continued.

"Well, he had on a brown kind of sweater, and tan twill pants."

"No coat?"

"Well, not of his own. He had on that fur thing that you all saw him in, here, the other day."

"So he had been out of the building."

"I can't say for sure."

Dave tilted his head at him slightly, and lowered his hands an inch, to give his whole face to Fishman. The look on it was not amused.

"Mr. Fishman, it would be a strange and impractical outfit for a man to wear some arctic fur, if he were only going down to the Williams' restaurant for a coffee or sandwich. Wouldn't it? Might we then surmise that he had been beyond the walls of the building?"

It hadn't been too clever of Fishman, and he seemed to know it. He looked down at the floor. Embarrassed. I was beginning to debate with myself whether or not I should spill it for him, but then he wasn't out of the stabbing pool yet, so I wanted to see how far he might try to run with leaving things out.

He shook his head at the floor, and admitted, "I suppose he had been out, Mr. DeGrabber."

Tired with that tangent, Scott got back on track.

"Ok, director. So Law get's back to the place, Turner stamps out the door, and Spencer's got his back side through a coffee table. Then what did you do?"

Dave tacked on, "Start with Mr. Law, please."

Fishman ran a hand over his mug, and pressed on.

"Law just kind of looked around at us and went back to his room." He looked at Dave, and received a silent blessing to go on. He did. "Cindy didn't seem like she thought much of Phillip, for his attempt at chivalry, and disappeared back down the hall. To her room, I suppose. Ally and I got Phillip to his feet and began cleaning up the remains of the table. Phillip was rattled. Ally reproached him for what he had tried to do. He waved her off and stormed off toward the pool room. We gathered up the table. Ally said she would go tell Robert about our plans for the evening. Uhm, also that she had a headache, and to check if he had any powders."

Even out of the corner of my eye, I could see him wince at the choice of word he'd ended up with. I made a little noise, to show what I thought of him for it.

Scott heard it, but I had wanted him to.

"What is it, Trait?"

I was matter of fact about it.

"Mr. Fishman, here. Confided in me, that he had been using Rob Law to procure drugs for Ally Lawrence, and that such a procurement had taken place that very day. He can probably tell us, but I imagine that's where Mr. Law had been."

Fishman took it well enough. He was as low in his chair as his shoulders and back could get him.

Scott swung over, and aimed a pencil eraser at him.

"Is this true, director? You've been paying Law to supply your girlfriend?"

"It is true."

"So that's where Law got that five bills we found?"

"I don't know for sure. I didn't pay him directly

for it. He was compensated for extras in his weekly stipend. He makes twice what the other non-actors do."

Fishman's chin was on his chest. Sunk right through his thin scarf. His voice was just a thin mutter. We still had some hours to get through.

"Then where'd he get the five hundred from?"

I decided to take that one, just to help get Fishman through to the end.

"Fishman told me, that he suspects Mr. Law was skimming cash off the top of what he was giving him for the buys, or I guess, what he was having added to his pay. He doesn't know much about that kind of purchase, and says he wouldn't know if the bag was light."

"Is that true?" Scott asked.

Fishman had to raise his head up to get the nod to work right.

"Ok. Ally is back picking up her delivery. What did you do?"

"I gathered up the table and carried it out. I started to go to the elevator, but didn't think the management would be too happy about me having broken furniture in my arms. I decided to go down the hall, to the stairwell that lets out by the alley. I threw it away there. It was so damn cold. I spotted a shop with some coats in the window, across the street, and decided to go and get one. That's when I bought that one I wore today."

He motioned back behind him. I looked back toward the doorway, and spied a brand new black leather duster. It was a strange choice, for my taste, but would probably look right at home on a cold LA night. That is, of course, provided he wasn't going to tell us that he then ran upstairs and stabbed Rob Law to death. In which case Chicago would be his last stop. At this point, nothing would have surprised me.

He didn't say that though. The rest of his report was a washout. He told that he had tried coats on for nearly two hours. Trying to decide between a brown wool thing, or the duster that he bought. He said he had also gone in for some heavy mittens, because all they had in the costume truck were thin deerskin gloves, that looked good on camera and left you as dexterous as you could be, before you got too cold. When he got back up with his haul, Ally was in high spirits behind the kitchen counter, telling Stanley Turner, who had returned, and was on the couch smoking, that Phillip was sorry for what he had done, and that they were all going to make up for it, and have a good time at the blues joint. Fishman's report of the rest of the evening was the same as mine, and even foggier overall.

Scott went around the horn, asking if we could think of anything else for the director to think about, but we were out. He told the officer that he could take Fishman back to his place, and they left. That left myself, Dave, and Scott in the office, with the seating all funny, in my opinion.

I asked, "You ready to switch out, detective?"

He crushed out his cigarette, and grinned at me.

"I've still got to book you, Trait." He was just adding comic relief though, and relinquished my chair. I took it and got settled, checking the message sheet, out of habit. Scott pulled the chair I had vacated right up close to the end of my desk, and motioned Dave to lean in. He reached into his coat and pulled out another small yellow envelope. He opened the flap and poured the contents onto my desk. Another .38 caliber brass casing.

I reached for my side drawer, and pulled out my own .38 to repeat the test that Dave had done. Scott stopped me.

"No need for that on this one. Already checked it myself. You can get it in, of course, but it's not like a fresh one. One of the lab guys got at it with a caliper too. It's been fired. Primer's shot and everything. The genuine article."

Dave seemed unimpressed.

"You found it on Mr. Law?"

"We did indeed."

Dave twisted his lip at the corner.

"The problem is clear enough. Did Law have it all along, or did his killer, possibly the killer of both men, plant it on him? I don't suppose we're fortunate enough to have fingerprints?"

Scott held the brass between two fingers, and shook his head at it.

"I swear, DeGrabber. I know that people have been caught by fingerprints, but I can't think of a time when they wouldn't have been caught without them. You know what I mean? It's like bad guy 101, that if you don't get caught red handed, or don't want to get caught right away, just keep a rag or some gloves in your pocket. Even still, there was a fingerprint on it. It belonged to our latest stiff, if he put it there on his own, then case closed on the Roker shooting, but now we've got a stabber loose. If his killer pressed his finger to it, then we're as stuck as we have been. I will say though, I'm beginning to like Fishman for this one. Maybe he killed Law for skimming that cash off him."

"And Law just happened to have the evidence of the first murder on him by coincidence?"

Scott exhaled. "I don't like that part either."

"John. What was Rob Law wearing when you saw him there in the bathroom?"

"That's an easy one. He had a navy blue jacket, like yours. Matching slacks, and a bright electric blue slick button up."

"So he had been informed of the night's theme, and was prepared to attend."

"What about a theme?" Scott asked.

I filled him in. "Ally got word around for everybody to wear blue to the Blues House."

Scott turned a palm up to me.

"But she had on a red dress."

"I noticed. It may be possible that the famous Hollywood actress likes to be the center of attention."

Scott feigned admiration.

"Wow, Trait. You could probably test through the whole academy on that catch alone." With his dig in, he continued. "I'm heading back to the station. We've got the rest of them scheduled to come in throughout the day and give us their versions of this. You two can have at them if we don't have them right then. Good luck."

With that, he got to his feet, gave us a parting nod, and headed out for the elevator. Scott doesn't like a fuss to be made over him, so he let himself out. I looked over to Dave, from my spot at the desk. He was staring a hole through the corner of his typewriter. He didn't look good, and I wondered if he had remembered to eat during his forty eight hour movie binge. I knew I hadn't, and with the amount of liquids I had consumed the night before, my guts were beginning to remind me. I announced that I would go hunt down some grub. Barbecue, hopefully, from a trailer down the street. The old black man that ran it made the best in town, and was often open for the after church crowd on Sundays. Dave didn't respond, so it would just be a double order of whatever I decided. He's never picky about eating.

With fruits of a successful expedition in hand, Dave and I dug into sandwiches with slaw, and beans. The bread worked wonders on my stomach. A couple of bites in, I thought we could use some atmosphere. I got over to our office radio, on top of the central file cabinet, along the back wall, and tuned it to the Bears game. I went back to my sandwich and listened to the call and thought to myself how glad I was that I was listening to it indoors, instead of taking it in from the stands with the freezing wind in my face. Dave didn't follow much football. I fielded a half dozen questions from him, about things like, "Why do they call one a full back, and another a half back?". That one did beat me too, because I've never understood why the half was behind the full. Seems like it should be the other way around. Not everyone can know everything. Dave also wondered aloud why there was no forward, since they had backs. Another good question, but I told him he might try basketball, since they had fewer positions to keep up with.

12

Most of Sunday was spent kicking around the office. A few ambitious reporters called for our thoughts on the latest slaying, or asked our opinion on whether the show should go on. Dave waxed poetically about film making to one guy. He had apparently formed a few ideas about the creative process. That, or he just liked giving a beat writer a tricky page of notes to sift through. As far as work went, Dave figured that our clients and suspects, had probably had a later night, and rougher morning, than even I had. With the police cleaning up, searching for clues, and asking everyone's life story, he was probably right. We decided to give them a chance to take some afternoon naps before we came in shaking trees. I asked Dave if he planned to take care of his face. He asked what for, so I just let it go. Our main idea was to figure out who went back with Rob, and when. Dave also wanted some more detail as to why Phillip Spencer had planted the bogus brass in Turner's pocket, and where did he get it. Did Rob Law help him, or is he handy in that sort of way himself? Around six o'clock we locked up, and headed around to the garage for

Shane Chastain

Dave's sedan.

The Sunday evening traffic wasn't much to speak of, and we got to the condo building in no time. Dave drove around the block twice trying to find a place to park. I kept telling him they had a valet all day every-day, but he didn't want to be a bother. Eventually he saw it was hopeless and stopped at the awning, and let the man take his car around.

As we entered, I remembered what I had thought of in my fog, as Douglas Leech had half carried me through the lobby the night before. I motioned to Dave for us to pop in Williams'. I got to the hostess and asked for the manager. Before she even got the whole message, I saw him coming toward me from across the dining room in a huff. He was an Italian fellow with slicked back hair, and he was gesturing toward the door with what I'll call, a good deal of pas-sion. There were a fair number of tables full of people eating, so he wasn't saying anything as he hurried our way. I put my hands up to him, apologetically, as he arrived. He started sternly.

"You, out. I won't have you in here again shoot-ing up the place."

"Hey, now. I didn't pull an triggers at all, pal. That was your Hollywood actress that did that. You know, the one that you put your best man on. Look." I took out my detective's license and showed it to him. "My partner and I, are investigating that shooting on the movie set. You've seen it in the papers?"

He said he had, and reached his hands out to gather more comments, but I stopped him.

"Good. I need to know, when she fired that shot in here the other night, did you find a bullet hole anywhere? It would have been in the ceiling."

He had calmed down a little, and handed the card back.

"No. No hole anywhere. What was she thinking? We had to give one older woman her bill for free. She had had such a shock. Not to mention the bill that you guys ran out on."

Now I got stern.

"Now listen, pal. I was prepared to pay that, and you ran us out the door." I pulled some bills out of my wallet and pushed them in his chest. "Here. You can't say John Trait runs out on his tab."

He had been the very man that ran us out that night, and now looked embarrassed for bringing it up. He took the money and handed it back to me, apologizing for losing his temper like he had. I accepted, though I felt that he had been within his rights to have run us out. It was poor of him to bring the bottle of champagne back up though, because at the prices they charged for pops at Williams', that bottle wasn't going to make much difference to their bottom line. We thanked him for his time, and retreated back into the lobby. On the way to the elevator Dave had a laugh about the whole thing. I couldn't blame him though.

He wasn't at risk of being branded a public nuisance, after all.

Dave knocked on the condo door, when we got off at the seventh floor. Walter Fishman opened up and let us in. They were all there, displaying varying degrees of misuse. Turner, Lawrence, and Wilson were all three on the couch, with Turner in the middle. He was smoking, as usual. At the back half of the room, was a kitchenette with a sink and counter, with some chairs around it. Phillip Spencer was sitting at one looking like an outcast. Over at the corner bar, was most of the motel crew. Doug was behind it, mixing drinks for Molly Fisher and Mark Macin, the better looking lighting boy. The mood in the place was low. Once we were inside, Walter spoke.

"I was just about to tell everyone about Steve's services." He turned from us, and spoke up to the group. "Everyone. Tomorrow, we may get word on whether or not we'll be able to continue our work here. I hope that we are able to, in honor of Steve and Robert's memory. Whether we do or not though, tomorrow at one, we have a visitation scheduled for Steve. After that, his body will be shipped back to Stockton, by train, for burial."

As though it was in the script, and rehearsed, Ally Lawrence put her head in her hands and began to sob. Cindy Wilson reached over the back of Turner and put a hand on her shoulder. Turner didn't make much of an expression at all, but I hadn't expected him to. Nobody spoke for a moment. Doug came around with a tray of shots from the bar, and passed them out to everyone. He held one for himself aloft, and invited them to have a drink in Steve's honor. A part of me was surprised Doug would care to make the gesture for the man that kept him on the outside looking in at his fellow thespians. I figured he must have just been trying to do it for the cheer of the group.

"We would like to talk to you, Mr. Spencer." It was Dave breaking the ice. He hadn't met, or seen, Phillip Spencer, so it was either context clues, or my description of him, that directed Dave right to his man.

Phillip let his arms fall down to his side, and tossed his head back. He let out some sort of groan.

"Fine. Let's do it in the pool room." He drug himself off the high chair, and trudged toward the double door. Dave made some excusatory gestures to the others as we followed him in.

In the corner of the room were a couple of good sized leather chairs. Spencer sank into one, and propped his head up with his hand. His determination to look dejected was getting on my nerves. He had been the one who tried to frame someone, and was lucky we weren't talking to him through bars. Now he acted like he was so upset that someone would ask him why he would make such an honorable play against his fellow man. Dave ignored the poor body language by taking the seat opposite our host, and assuming the same position. I leaned on the side of the pool table, and got a notepad ready.

"What compelled you to put that shell casing in Mr. Turner's jacket?" Dave asked.

Spencer's tongue played on his teeth for a moment while he thought of an answer, that I assume, wouldn't sound childish.

"I thought he deserved it." He said. I shudder to think how bad his rejected answers must have sounded. He continued. "He doesn't care anything about Cindy. You know? She was just available. These actors have a way with women that men like us can't compete with. He wants Ally, but since the director has her, he thinks he can just take whatever's in reach. It's vile. He's the one that pulled the trigger anyway. Shot Steve dead as he lay in the street. It makes as much sense for him to pay as anyone else."

I had a million questions and comments. There was no, "Men like us.", in my mind, because men like me don't go around trying to frame people, or lie to the police. Also, I didn't believe he had any idea what Stanley Turner cared about. For all he knew, he and Cindy Wilson might have as good a thing going as any other. Furthermore, this idea that actors were just waving their hands, and stealing someone's woman, didn't strike me as saying much for his own self confidence, or for the women's ideas of loyalty. The only thing vile here, in my mind, were Phillip Spencer's nihilistic feelings about love and romance. That's to say nothing of his ideas about assignment of guilt. If someone cut his brakes, and he barreled into a group of pedestrians, did he want the public to hold him solely responsible, instead of the saboteur?

I was trying to decide which side to start on first, but Dave had other ideas. He bypassed the philosophizing entirely.

"Where did you get the casing that you put in the coat pocket? Did anyone help you to remove the bullet?"

"Friday, after your man here came to talk to me, I came up with the idea. I went out and bought a small box of .38s. I wasn't sure how I wanted to do it, but I went to Rob's trailer because he had the tools and a bench in there, and pulled a few out with the pliers. I had some trouble not nicking the brass, but I finally got one that I thought would pass. I even pressed a dent into the round thing on the bottom, but I guess it wasn't good enough. Anyway, I put it inside of a glove, in my coat pocket. Next, I waited till Stanley was out, and went in and put it in the pocket of one of the jackets he had in his room. Then all I had to do was go back and claim it, to take it back to the costume trailer, and tell what I'd found to the police."

Just a piece of work this guy. Just a stoned cold frame up. I had to ask.

"Have you told this to the police?"

He shook his head.

"No. When they asked me about it last, I told

them someone else must have put it there, and I'd just happened to find it."

I told him plainly.

"You're going to go to jail."

He didn't seem to care though. He just sat there looking petulant. That's what I'd decided it was. He hadn't gotten his way with Cindy Wilson, and he had made up his mind to make everyone as miserable as he was. I guess he thought, if Turner went down for the murder, then Cindy would have no other option but him. Gutless.

There was a point that I had hoped Dave hadn't misplaced. Always batting 1.000, he had it queued up.

"Mr. Spencer. You know that Steve Roker also had a relationship with Miss Wilson. I don't suppose you have any other confessions you'd like to make, as to how you may have tried to resolve that difficulty?"

"You asking me if I put that round in Turner's gun?"

"I am."

"How would I have done that, DeGrabber? I'm the costume man. Rob loaded the weapons."

Dave was right on him.

"And now Mr. Law is dead. Found stabbed thirty feet from here, with the real casing in his jacket pocket. A not small amount of cash was found in his possession. Did you pay him to load and unload Mr.

Turner's prop gun, with deadly effect? Then, did you kill him in fear of his outing you? Thereby eliminated your two chief romantic competitors."

Spencer's head now held itself aloft again. His hands gripped at the arms of his chair. He was enraged, and gritted his teeth.

"I did not. It might've been good if I had." He hissed through his teeth.

Dave was still sitting, with his own head propped up, as though he was watching a slow television program.

"Where did Robert Law get the $500 dollars?"

"I don't know."

"Was it Fishman?"

"I said, I don't know."

"Steve Roker?"

"Dammit, I told you, I don't know!" He slapped both arms of the chair, and nearly screamed it.

"Thursday, earlier in the day, shooting a scene in which Miss Lawrence was to fire on Mr. Turner, did she use her personal handbag in that scene, or another from your trailer?"

The sudden shift in topic, and Dave's completely unaffected tone, caused Spencer's head to jerk back. He stared for a moment. He may have been considering the possibility of trying to tear Dave's head from his body, but it turned out he was just thinking of the answer.

"She used the bag that she's been carrying for the last month. The whole troupe, especially the talent, uses the costume trailer as their personal wardrobe."

"After the scenes, do you make any checks of the bags, or clothes?"

"I do not."

Dave said to me, without looking, "We'll have to find out from Detective Scott, if his men found Miss Lawrence's pistol during their initial search."

I nodded and made a note of it.

Dave dismissed our man.

"Thank you for your time, Mr. Spencer."

Phillip Spencer jerked his head back again at the sudden termination of his interview, looked to me, then back at Dave, got up with a noise, and took three big steps across to the door, and went out.

Dave said to me. "Get me Ally Lawrence."

I stepped out and got her. She was still irrigating a piece of cotton. I sat her in front of Dave, where Spencer had been. Tired of standing, I carried one of the tall pool stools over, and set up around Dave's elbow. He was sat low in his chair with his feet out, nearly to Ally's. His lapel was all crooked, and his fingers were interlaced at his middle. He watched Ally dab at the corners of her eyes for a moment, then got started.

"Miss Lawr-"

"Who is this, John?" Ally interrupted.

Dave pushed the starter again.

"My name is David DeGrabber, Miss Lawrence. I need to ask you a number of questions. Some, I fear, you may think to be inappropriate in their personal nature. I assure you, I mean you no further discomfort, but it will be necessary to ask them, if we're to remove a violent murderer from your midst." She nodded and twisted her rag in her hands. Dave continued. "Where is your nickel .32 pistol?"

She seemed taken aback by that.

"Well, it's in my bag."

"Can you show it to me?"

"I can go get it." She started to stand, but Dave held her.

"No, Miss Lawrence. John can get it." He shot me a look. As I went toward the door Ally told me it was on her bed. The room was down a little hallway that started toward the end of the mini bar. It was the master suite. The same bag that I'd seen her with my whole time knowing her, was there on a huge double bed. I retrieved it, and went back to the pool room, ignoring the curious looks I got from the others, as I passed through the main room.

"Here it is." I said. Handing it to her.

She popped open the clasp and looked inside. It was just a small purse. Not much bigger than was needed to hold her pistol and her compact, but she rifled through it anyway, as if the weapon was underneath a checkbook. Her brow furrowed, and she stated,

"It's not here. Where could it have gone?"

I still had it in my pocket and now pulled it out and held the small automatic in my palm.

"Did you take it out?" She asked.

"I took it from you Friday night, after you fired it in the dining room of Williams'.

She smiled, as if remembering something nice.

"Oh, yes. We went there after dancing. I fired a shot? Was anyone hurt?"

Dave took back over.

"No, Miss Lawrence. The only thing disturbed seems to have been your fellow revelers peace."

I added on.

"It seemed that your gun was still loaded with a movie blank in the chamber, from your scenes the day before. The rest of the magazine is full of real bullets though."

She looked concerned.

"I don't see how that could be. Robert swapped my prop gun out for my personal one like always."

I looked over to Dave. He was looking back.

I eased into it.

"Well, Ally. Friday night, at the restaurant, you insisted that the gun in your bag just had blanks in it. Now you're telling us that you expected it to be the loaded one."

She was harder to get a read on than Turner. Turner just put one face on at a time, and you weren't sure if he had put it there himself, or not. Ally was all over the place. Now she looked exactly like a confused person would look, but there was no telling, by my eye, if it had gotten there honestly. She got it worked out though.

"I remember now. I never gave Robert my personal gun. It's been in my suitcase since we got to Chicago. Those scenes Thursday were a mess. Steve kept getting the timing wrong, and we were shooting and shooting. After a while all our ears were ringing, and Robert said he was running low on blanks, so Walter said we would wrap and come back to it. I thought I had given the gun back to Robert, but that night, when the police found it in my bag during the search, I figured Rob must have missed it."

"Where is your suitcase, Miss Lawrence?" Dave asked.

She told us, and I went and got it. It was in a closet in the master bedroom. This time I told the onlookers in the main room, that we were setting up a flee market, as I lugged the case through. With it procured, we set it on the pool table and flipped the latches up. There amongst the linens and lace unmentionables, was another pearl gripped nickel .32. It had a little more wear on the finish than the one I had bore for the last two days. It was also full of live rounds, with one ready in the pipe. That didn't exactly solve the mystery. If anything it made it an even darker soup. Who had racked a single blank into the prop pistol, and then let her keep it with her. Maybe she had done it herself, but the only way I could see that adding up, was if she had meant to kill Stanley Turner. Dave had his face screwed up, but only enough that you could tell if you knew to look for it, so I figured he was having the same conversation with himself. We had other things to cover though, and much like anesthesia, you can't keep your patient under, and workable, forever. We got back to our previous positions, and Dave asked some more questions.

"We need to know exactly what happened after Mr. Turner pushed Mr. Spencer into the coffee table, and you went back to Mr. Law's room. I must also preface this by telling you that we do know the nature of Mr. Law's errands for Mr. Fishman, as well as your partaking of his haul."

She bit her lip and looked at the floor from the corner of her eye. Finally she answered in a weak voice.

"I went back to get my head right. Rob had just come back with the weeks worth."

Dave was calm, but quick.

"He was alive at that time."

Her eyes came back up with some surprise.

"Yes. He was fine. He asked me what had happened and I told him. We got cheered up, then I told him about the night's theme, and went to smooth things over between Phillip, and Stanley. I talked to Phillip first, but he was being a stick in the mud about it, so then I went to talk to Cindy. Stanley wasn't around."

"When did Mr. Turner return?" Dave asked.

"I don't know. I stayed in Cindy's room, and we worked on our makeup for a while. When I came back out I think he was on the couch."

"When was the next time you saw Mr. Law?"

She put on a grim face and responded.

"When we got back from the Blues House. He never showed up so I thought maybe he had fallen asleep, what with the police keeping him the night before. There he was with the knife sticking out of him. It was terrible."

The water works looked to be starting up again, so Dave worked quickly.

"Only a final question, Miss Lawrence. Before you left, did anyone check to see if Mr. Law was ready, or coming along at all?"

She thought.

"Walter called for him from the hallway, and then stepped in and looked in the bedroom. Maybe he thought he was using the bathroom, or had already gone down with the others. I don't know."

It was as good an answer as any. I wouldn't have put it past Walter Fishman to have seen the body and acted like he hadn't, except that he had looked so pitiful in our office that morning. I feel like I would have noticed if he had recently gotten that kind of shock, when I'd saw him at the blues club.

Dave sent Ally out, and asked for her to send Stanley Turner back to us. We sat for about five minutes with no action at the doorway, so I poked my head out to see what the hold up was. Turner was still there on the couch below a haze of his own making. I called to him, and he turned around.

"You coming, Turner?"

He coughed and answered back.

"No."

Dave had heard the message and got to his feet. He sidled by me into the main room. He stopped at the end of the couch and looked down at Turner. Dave said,

"Where did you go after you left here yesterday, after pushing Mr. Spencer?"

Turner ignored him. Dave hates to be ignored.

I've told you that if someone clams up, he likes to guess. He worked up a doozy.

"I believe, Mr. Turner, that you stepped out only for a moment. Possibly only outside the door. You peeked in to check that no one was in the main room, took a knife from the kitchenette, and entered Mr. Law's room where he was preparing in his bathroom. There you stabbed him to death, and made it back to this couch before anyone else returned from their rooms to see you."

Turner hurried to his feet and met Dave face to face. They were nearly the same height, but Turner probably had twenty pounds and a couple of years on Dave. It seemed Turner liked to do a lot of spitting on people when he had a disagreement. He blew a bit of smoke out of the side of his mouth, removed his cigarette, and positioned his head to hock up something for Dave, as he had done to Phillip Spencer. Dave wasn't having it. He moved nothing but his right arm, and chopped Turner in his throat. Coughing and wheezing ensued. Turner's face now had affixed to it the look of a man beside himself with rage. He balled a right hand down by his belt, and began to turn his hips to deliver a blow. Dave brought his left up open, and connected flush with Turner's ear and the side of his head. Dave hadn't moved much, but must have struck cleanly, because Turner fell into the couch next to him. He had a knee on the couch, a foot on the floor, and both hands on the back for balance. He looked back at Dave, who was standing straight and flat footed, like a statue. Dave's face showed no particular expression, which I thought to be unnerving.

It seemed that Turner had found it likewise. He turned around and resumed his seat, reach for a fresh cigarette, and said,

"I went down to Williams' for a drink, and then walked over to Lakeshore and had some smokes. I was gone a couple hours I guess."

"Thank you, Mr. Turner." Dave said that as if his question had been answered without the slightest protest.

The rest of the crew had just stood gawking. It can often be a quiet scene when men are getting slapped with open hands, and this was certainly one of them. Dave said to Fishman, as we made our way for the door, that he would be in touch, and we left.

Off the elevator, on the ground floor, we stopped by Williams' again, and parted with ten of our client's dollars to the bartender, for confirmation that he had indeed seen Turner the day before. He had. Said he had taken two double scotch's, smoked four cigarettes, paid with an even twenty, and left. Total time of stay: twelve minutes approximately. That was kind of frustrating. The rest of the alibi was simply unprovable. It was Sunday, and the Saturday evening sidewalk people were not the same as the Sunday bunch. By next weekend, nobody would have remembered that they had been walking on Lakeshore, in the cold, much less whether or not they'd seen a chain smoking actor.

We had the car brought around, and made the block. Dave wanted to check Fishman's alibi at the coat store, but we found it was closed on Sunday. It was a formality really. Ally had spilled that Fishman was the last one to head toward Law's room. It's conceivable that he could have had the knife up his jacket sleeve, walked in there and managed a deft jab with it. That of course, would again be granting the director a good amount of acting ability to get through the night as though everything was fine. Also, what did he kill him for?

I said a lot of that stuff out loud, as we drove away from downtown. Dave didn't comment as such, but made a series of short grunts. Likely piecing it all together in his quiet way. I asked what the plan was as we turned off the trail to the office. Dave said he had another film to watch, and some things to show me back at his place. It didn't involve drinks or dancing, so I made no protest.

13

Once again slid into The DeGrabber Theatre, and this time having slept a bit, and imbibed none, I took the liberty of straightening up the place. Even more pop cans had been added to the collection by the couch. I gathered them up and got myself around the big screen that blocked the kitchen to throw them away. Flies were working on the contents of a pizza box that sat open on the kitchen table. It was a pepperoni, with only a single slice missing. Dave must have forgotten it in his single mindedness.

"Were you expecting company?" I called back.

I guess he didn't hear me. I shooed the bugs and closed the box. Though the pizza didn't exactly look appetizing, and maybe it was only the alcohol that my system was working through, I decided to check the refrigerator for something to add to the works. As always seemed to be the case at Dave's house, it was a washout; or you might say it could have stood a washout. Inside was nothing more than a crusty milk bottle, half a sandwich, and a bottle of ketchup. I shook my head at it.

With the place marginally more livable, I went around the obstructions and joined Dave on the couch. He had a fresh reel on and was spinning it ahead.

"We not want to see the beginning?" I asked, taking a seat.

"This is the one I told you about on the phone last night."

"I was under duress. Remind me."

"It's called, 'The Deft Touch', and it stars Stanley Turner, as quite a young man. In it he plays a pickpocket and sleight of hand artist."

I was making out what he was getting at, but it seemed like a stretch. He found the spot he was looking for and set it to play.

In the scene, a baby faced Stanley Turner stood in a room, with a larger man in a busy outfit, and a woman on his other side. He was making a demonstration.

"You see, Sara." He said. "It's all a matter of misdirection. It's about making contact, that seems incidental, while you work on the watch, or the eye glasses. Maybe even the hat. And carefully, but quickly, the belt." As he listed the items, he stepped around the large man, placing one hand on him in a friendly and casual sort of way, and with the other, dexterously unclasping his watch band, untying his tie, plucking his glasses, and snatching his hat. In the span of a couple passes around, he had removed, and himself donned, all the items. The big man did a double take at Stanley, and the girl, Sara, gave a little applause. Dave stopped the picture.

"I mean, it's the movies, Dave. That doesn't show us anything." I complained. I felt like I was back in the theatre downtown, having my knowledge of ballistics insulted again by, 'The Golden Talon'. I crossed my arms, and looked over to Dave.

I was dumbfounded. David DeGrabber had both of my shoes on top of his head. He was sitting there, arms crossed, face looking bored, like always, with both my size nines atop his mop. One on top of the other. I opened my mouth to speak, but he beat me to it.

"John, taking on a role can often require a great deal of study and practice. Not to mention that many talented people in Hollywood possess a whole host of talents. How many times have you seen a film in which the leading man, or lady, break into song and dance? I can show you examples of all of our suspects doing just that, among other interesting skills. For instance, did you know that Cindy Wilson, known to you as a makeup person, not only acts, but is a capable puppeteer and ventriloquist?"

I told him I didn't know that, but logged another gripe. "Dave. Turner didn't get the bullet into Steve Roker's chest by sleight of hand. Even if he got it in the gun, right under Rob Law's nose, how did he get it out, and another blank casing back in?"

For that, Dave dug around for another film. He skipped ahead, and explained how in this one, Stanley Turner played a sidewalk shark in New York. Dave showed me three different scenes. They worked like this: Turner was running a shell game, with the three cups and the rock under one of them. He smoked constantly. The crook was, after he let somebody win a few times, he'd be near the end of his cigarette. He'd shuffle the cups around a bit, start to run them with one hand, and with the other, he'd take out a pack of smokes from his breast pocket. In the last scene it was revealed what he was doing. He'd take the rock from out of the cup at the edge of the table, swap hands, and place it into the smoke pack. The cup guess would of course be wrong. Then he'd go back to the same pocket for the lighter. He'd bring the pack and the lighter back out, get the rock back in his hand, invisibly to the viewer, and make it appear under a different cup.

A scenario was beginning to take shape in my head. It was no longer quite as great a span but still a good reach, in my mind.

"So, you're saying he pinches some used brass from Law's pouch, and keeps it in his smokes-"

"At any time before. And he could have just kept that in his pocket." Dave added.

"Ok. So he finds a good scene, swaps a round out with the pick pocket move, shoots Roker, then what?"

"Take out your pistol."

He was lucky I had brought it. I'd put my snub nosed .38 in my jacket pocket, with the expectation of returning Ally's gun. I pulled it out.

"You didn't pinch this along with the shoes?"

Dave gave the smallest grin, and said, "That would have been too personal."

He took the pistol from me, and held it out in front of him.

"Let's pretend that Rob Law has just reloaded this with blanks for the next take. I've put a live round in, by some simple misdirection. The director calls for action. I fire a shot. Bang. Fortune smiles on me, lessening my need for caution and execution a great deal. You have walked out and ruined the take. I fire the second shot, as normal. I know that Douglas Leech's eyes will be on his clapper and most others will be on you."

Dave flipped the cylinder open, and pressed the ejector, as he explained.

"I open the cylinder, bump the ejector, causing my two used casings to protrude, and hold the gun in one hand. With my other, I reach for my cigarettes and lighter, like always. My hand now holds the spent brass of the second shot. I put it into my cigarette pack, take the blank brass from my pocket, put it back in the gun, and close the cylinder." He shut the cylinder with the one hand, so that it closed quietly. "Now, with the brass reasonably hidden, my man dead or dying, and the paraphernalia of my habit in hand as usual, Rob Law takes the gun from me, and begins to load it, like always."

I had slipped my shoes back on, while keeping my eyes and ears on Dave. I sat back on the couch and thought for a moment.

"I tell you, Dave. If you had just come up with all that, without the pictures, it would be outrageous. I don't suppose there's anything in that stack of movies that would tell us, for sure, that Stanley Turner even knows how to work a pistol. Much less set the wheel on a live round, in the dark, with gloves on."

Dave was unbothered. He was starting to seem excited now, which I find to be unnerving, yet auspicious.

"Nothing so specific. I realize that the police, and it seems yourself, believe Mr. Turner's aversion to firearms puts him out of it. I believe he hasn't done any shooting, but if we could get him to tell us, I think we'd learn that he's done a great deal of dry practice."

"Dry practice?"

"Calisthenics, John. In the same way that a martial artist practices his forms, so too has Stanley Turner ingrained, privately, his loading and unloading method, and on film for us to see, his accuracy. It is clear, in every scene that Stanley Turner shoots at someone, that he aims straight at their heart."

I laid my head to the side, in tepid agreement, and said, "Alright, Dave. Let's say you've got it. It doesn't take a criminal mastermind to know to go all thumbs if somebody came to them with the idea of all this sleight of hand stuff. How do we prove that Turner's been lying from the start? Also, does that mean he killed Rob Law too, and what for?"

Dave pushed my pistol back to me, and considered for a moment. Finally he spoke.

"Your second question is not difficult. I'm quite certain, that if Turner killed Roker, then he also killed Law, as I illustrated to him at the condo."

"But why?"

"Because he supplied Ally Lawrence with her drugs. I don't imagine Mr. Fishman will be safe long, should he seek a new source to meet her needs, now that Law is dead."

I shook my head.

"I don't know, Dave. It doesn't seem like sound reasoning to kill everyone that your addict ex-lover gets her stuff from."

Dave nodded.

"It doesn't, but it is the only motive that fits for all of it. Besides, it's poor reasoning to murder anyone. Isn't it? Can you think of any idea that resolves all the points?"

They were a good couple of questions, and I didn't have an answer for either of them. The first one, about the reasonability of murder, was well beyond my pay grade. As far as the second went, I thought, if we could get some pressure on Turner about his gun handling, then maybe he'd break on the whole thing. That seemed like our only way to get anyone. It looked like a long shot to me.

Dave put on what he said was the last film of the bunch, one he hadn't seen yet, and we had it on as we kicked ideas around in our own heads. It was only a movie featuring Douglas Leech in a minor role, and nobody else we were looking for. Dave had just got it to be thorough.

I stayed for the whole picture, all the way through the credits. We didn't speak any more that night. I just kept trying to think of a way to out Turner. When I would try an idea out in my mind, and hit a wall, I'd swap to trying to think up another better suspect. No luck, which is a shame. Aside from the spitting on people, which was a serious mark against him, I liked Turner well enough. Even still, there was no denying that Dave had made a strong case for the means, motive, and opportunity. Dave went ahead and drove me back to my place.

Nothing happened Monday morning, worth telling. Dave beat me to the office, the papers talked more about the stabbing, and so we decided on a fishing trip. Not the sort where we bundle up and pick and shovel ourselves a hole in the ice somewhere. Fishing, is what Dave called it, when we would sit in the office, at the ready, when nothing else was on the books, and wait for the phone to ring, or a knock at the door. Sessions would be a minimum of two hours, and if I didn't decide to turn the radio on, they might have been spent in total silence. There was lunch in there somewhere, but it was largely a boring day.

News did come in the afternoon. The evening paper reported that the city councilmen had sided with mine and Scott's logic on the movie shoot; since everyone had to stay around anyway, they may as well press on. Now they would need someone to stand in for both Roker and Law. I got on the phone with Fishman, at the condo, to see what he thought of the news. He sounded haggard, and told me that a couple of men were on the way from California to cover the parts. I asked him if he had remembered to tell them to dress warm, but he didn't seem to get it.

After a whole weekend of parties and nightlife, the prospect of a quiet evening struck me as mundane. I decided to see what the motel crew had going on. I got Douglas Leech on the horn, and he invited me back to the pool hall, saying he and the crew there were going to have a few drinks, and make a sendoff to the little dive bar, because they would all be moving into the condo on Tuesday. I found my way over that evening, and continued my recent dominance of billiards. The older men that we had tussled with were back too, but decided it was better to keep their comments to themselves this time. I made sure to talk in their direction, when I praised Doug for covering the door of the murder scene.

I called it an early night from the pool hall, and headed back to the office for one last message check before heading home. Sid had already gone by then, so I worked the elevator myself. Entering the office, I walked into crowd.

Dave was standing in front of our desks, with Ben Scott beside him. In front of them, turning their heads around to take me in as I entered, were seven uniformed female police officers.

"What's going on in here?" I asked, hanging my coat and hat on the rack.

Dave answered, "A talent casting. Ladies, this is my associate, John Trait. He'll be assisting us."

I made my way around the women, and got to my seat.

"What are we doing, anyway?"

14

The meeting went late into the evening. Most of the gang of agents weren't required for the duration. I could tell you the plan Dave laid out that night to Ben and I, and how he had lines picked out for all the women to repeat. Even go into to all the different ways that Ben found to object, at various points, or I can just show you what we came up with. The next morning started with some phone calls that turned out to be for confirmation of things that Dave had tentatively arranged while I had been on the pool tables. Everything was a go. All that was left to do was to wait for night fall. In that time of year we didn't have long. I was buzzing and ready to start around five thirty, just as what small bit of sun there was ducked below the buildings outside our office window. Days later, just two hours, at seven thirty, I headed down to kick things off.

It was a, "synchronize your watches", sort of job. I got off the elevator and knocked on the condo door at 8 sharp. Fishman opened up and I told him I was there to ask Ally Lawrence some more questions. He said she was out, but I told him I'd wait, because

I needed to smooth things over with Turner also. I asked if he would fetch Turner for me, and he did. I stayed by the door, near where the telephone was. Turner came across looking not too happy to see me.

"What do you want, Trait?" He sounded ready for bear.

"Easy, pal. I wanted to come by and make sure you were alright. I hear you're gonna get to make your red carpet walk, with this picture, after all."

He lightened up a bit.

"Well, thanks, John. I'm no worse for wear. I probably shouldn't have lost my head like I did last night. You all are just trying to work. Smoke?"

"Sure. I gotta say, Stan. It's tough to go to bat for a man that goes around spitting at people. You oughta get another move."

He chuckled.

"Maybe you can show me how DeGrabber worked that move he put on me."

The phone rang.

Stanley removed his cigarette, blew some smoke, excused himself to me, and picked up. I was just a few feet away and caught a bit of it. It was a woman's voice. Loud and under a strain. Stanley shouted some questions at the receiver, yelled for Ally, and then I heard the line go dead.

"What's wrong?" I asked.

He turned a circle toward me and back to the phone, and began to dial a number as he explained.

"It's Ally. She's in trouble. Said someone had her at the docks. Some kind of warehouse. An importer. I'm calling the police."

I got close and put my finger on the switch to stop his call. I talked to him low, so the others wouldn't hear.

"Listen, Stan. She's probably gone to re-up. I know you want to look out for her, but if you get the police after her for this, they might decide what she's into is worth making a fuss over. Up to now, they've let this stuff go, since you all are just passing through, but it could ruin her. Let's call DeGrabber. He's connected over in that area with this sort of thing. He probably can even think of where she went for the stuff. You've got some money?"

He sat the handset back in its place, and nodded.

"Ok. How about a gun? Just in case."

He nodded again, and returned his cigarette to his mouth. He started for his overcoat, there by the door, and motioned me to follow. We slid out and skipped the elevator for the stairs. He spoke as we started down.

"I'm going to borrow something from the prop trailer. There's a compartment where Law kept the live rounds, under the workbench."

"In the floor?"

"Yeah."

We came out onto the street, and I followed him down the alley. We stopped at a garage, a few hundred yards down, and went in. There were a few trailers that I hadn't seen since all this had started there in a row of spaces. He took a key from his pocket and opened the door to the props trailer. He climbed up, and ducked under the work bench.

"Hand me a screwdriver." He said.

I was keeping a lookout, but now got in and passed the utensil to him. I heard a little pop, and he sat a couple of boxes of rounds on the workbench. He stood up and looked over them.

"Dammit. All .32. Spencer must have taken the others."

I started looking around.

"I guess you'll have to use Ally's prop gun."

He voiced his agreement by pulling a drawer handle and producing the shiny nickel automatic. He loaded the magazine, inserted it in the grip, and ran the slide. A blank ejected onto the workbench. Now ready to fire, he dropped it into his pocket. We shut the door, not bothering to lock back up, and headed for the street. There I found a pay phone, and explained the situation to Dave. He said he would meet us down by the lake, and gave me a street lamp, in front of a Coke billboard, where we would find him. We hailed a cab, and told the driver to step on it.

"I don't know about your friend DeGrabber." Turner said, as we shifted through the downtown streets. He had smoked five cigarettes since we had left the condo. A high rate, even for him. He was nervous, so I tried to reassure him.

"Dave doesn't take anything personal. It's his one major flaw. Besides," I pointed out the cab window. "look at all those warehouses. If we don't know which one imports the kind of thing that Ally was looking for, then they might decide to export her before we find her."

"You mean, like for a ransom?"

"All kinds of things. We've got the mob here, you know? Here we are. Let us out here, driver."

The cab pulled over to the curb and we disembarked. The wind blowing off the lake took our breath away as we stepped out. It was well below freezing, and had been for some time. The lake ice went out for about a hundred yards, and beyond that you could tell the water was just slush. I looked around, and spotted Dave's sedan.

"This way." I motioned for Turner to follow.

We piled into Dave's car. I got in the passenger seat, and Turner in the back.

"Where do you think she is?" Turner's voice cracked a little.

Dave tilted his head forward.

"There. That blue importer's warehouse would be the mostly likely place. I've had dealings with them before. They don't take female clients. It was foolish of her to go alone."

"She just got some stuff on Saturday. I don't know why she would be out after it again so soon." Turner worried aloud.

Dave explained it away.

"The mind of an addict can be unpredictable. The possibility of her supply being cut off likely led her to seek a new avenue preemptively."

"Let's go in and get her. I've got two thousand dollars with me."

Dave didn't answer with words. He opened his door, and began to hurry across the street. We spilled out of our doors, and got on his heels.

Dave led us around to the back of the building. Ducking behind pallet stacks and crates of goods as we went. Finally we arrived at a side door. It was metal, and had a fixture for a light above, but no bulb. Dave tried the knob. It was unlocked. We all took a breath, as if preparing for a deep dive. That was when I blew it.

It was Dave, at the door, then Turner, then myself. I leaned on the corner of the building and bumped a tall metal pole. It, and a few like it, came crashing down in a loud clatter, from where they were leaned along the side of the building. Even with the noise of the wind, it carried around the stockyard. We didn't move a muscle, and only listened to determine if I had botched the whole rescue. After a moment, with no alarms audibly raised. Dave motioned us to go on in.

He turned the knob and swung the door open slowly. We crept in. It was dark, save for a light toward the middle. The room was massive, and there were shelves all around; all the way up to the ceiling, piled with goods. Lamps, sculptures, and crates of all sizes were on them. We began working our way around to the right, being careful not to bump anything as we crept down the narrow aisle. We picked our way around the corner, and Dave started us up a new row, going toward the light. A few steps in, Turner was struck from behind. We all went down. Next there was some dragging around.

15

It was hard to say how long I had laid there on the cold concrete floor before Turner began to stir. My eyes opened. The three of us were much closer to the middle of the room now, where the one light shown down from above. Turner came to with a jerk, but seeing what he had in front of him, quickly settled down. Before him, on the floor, was his automatic pistol. Just out of arms reach. Beyond that, some fifteen feet, was a man in a dark coat, with his hat pulled low. He had his back to us, and was nailing the top down on a large wooden shipping crate. Muffled kicks and cries from a woman could be heard from within. Beside the box the man was working on, were two more with their tops off. Presumably waiting for us, or our remains.

Turner made his move without warning. He scrambled forward and to his feet, picking up the .32 as he did. He leveled it at the man in the coat, and fired four times. The man fell in a heap over the crate, and slumped into the floor, his hammer falling with a clatter onto the concrete. Now Turner began to make his way toward the crate.

"Don't go any further, Mr. Turner." Dave was up on one knee, to my left. He sounded deadly serious. Turner stopped and turned to him.

He motioned to the box. "Come on, DeGrabber. We've got to get her out."

Dave got to his feet and stepped closer.

"We will free Miss Lawrence soon enough. It appears that fortune has smiled upon my partner and I. Unfortunately, it has happened at your expense."

Turner stepped to Dave. They were standing face to face.

"What are you talking about?" Turner seethed.

Dave was precise in his tone.

"You have presented us with an opportunity that we can literally not afford to miss. We know what you've done this past week in defense of Miss Lawrence. I now offer you a trade to defend her once more."

Turner brought the silver pistol up to Dave's temple. His hand shook with rage.

"I'll show you a piece of what I've done for her." He threatened.

In a flash Dave shot forward from his hips and struck Turner in the mouth with his head. As Turner went back Dave brought one hand to the pistol, and the other to the side of Turner's wrist. The gun came loose, and now Dave had it. He turned it on Turner and explained what he wanted.

"I would very much like you to show me what it is that you have done in Miss Lawrence's defense. I want it in writing. You were very clever. The way you prepared to make the switch. If you had only left the shell casing in the prop gun, then you might not have had to deal with Mr. Law the way you did. Perhaps you overthought it all. Maybe you thought you could do it and no one be held responsible."

"Dave, what the hell are you doing?" I protested.

Dave turned his head my direction. "John, it's the only way for us to collect our fee. I'm no prouder of this method than you are, but it is the only way."

Turner spoke defiantly.

"What do you think you're going to do, DeGrabber? Threaten me at gunpoint? You know that sort of confession would never hold up."

Dave shook his head.

"No, Mr. Turner. You have shot and killed a man with Ally Lawrence's gun. She's here. In that box. She had come here seeking her drugs, and they are doubtless to be on the man you shot. We will arrange it so that she is convicted of killing this man. We'll say we witnessed the whole thing. Swear to it, if necessary. We can say that we were tailing the both of you. Maybe we have been anyway. You wouldn't know."

Turner looked exactly like a man that was scared now, and I didn't think it was an act this time. He raised his voice to Dave.

"No one will believe that."

Dave stayed calm.

"Will they not? You've been the suspect of two murders this week. She is drug addict. Further, she fired this same weapon, in public, just a few nights ago. The entire city's opinion of you and your company is low. Also, Detective Scott is our friend, and allows our word to carry a good deal of weight. They would never believe we blackmailed you for a confession. Even now they consider to charge you with murder anyway."

There were some more noises from the box. Turner was beginning to crack.

"Dammit, we have to let her out." Turner turned toward the box, but Dave's voice held him.

"No. You will tell us, now, what you did, how and why." Turner had stopped, and Dave shouted past him. "We'll be right with you, Miss Lawrence. Hold tight."

A muffled, "Ok.", came back.

Turner looked to me for an ally.

"Are you in on this, John?"

I shook my head in disgust.

"I've got to be, Stan. We're starving out here, and we know you did it. You're the only one it all fits for."

I got earnest. "Don't let Ally go down for this, after all you've done for her."

I was surprised, and had to hide it, but Stanley Turner's shoulders dropped, and he suddenly looked far too old to play anything but a washed up actor. He was giving up.

He slumped down to his knees, and began to spill it.

"I did kill Roker. I hated him before he ever got with Ally. He was terrible to all the women. He didn't have any respect for them. Ally was too far though. Once he got his hooks in her, he just played with her. She's been destroying herself. I wish I had done it before he got to her."

"Explain it." Dave sounded unmoved.

"It came to me as soon as I saw that scene in the script. We were all in the condo, working through the whole picture, when we first got to town. I had dreamed of shooting Roker. When I saw there was a scene that I would shoot him dead, I suggested that we add the killing shot. My idea was that I wouldn't miss that way. I didn't either. I've always been slick. I swapped the real round, right under Rob's nose, and pinched a fired blank from his pouch too."

"We've seen your skill, in your films." Dave put in.

"Yeah. It was easy. I had practiced the move for hours getting ready for that moment. That night, when John stepped into the shot, I thought, this is it. Roker will be gone, and then I can steal her away from Fishman. That wouldn't be any problem. I shot him, and put the brass in with my smokes."

"Rob Law."

Turner looked up as if he had to think of who that name belonged to. After a deep breath, he went on.

"Rob. I confronted him after the police found that money. He wouldn't tell me where he got it, so I started trying to eavesdrop on him. I heard Fishman put in the order, and that was when I decided it had to stop. I wasn't gonna kill Rob, at first, but after I got so hot at Phillip I thought, what the hell. I'd already killed once. You know, DeGrabber, it feels good, in a way, to tell you all this. Can we let Ally out now?"

He sounded a mix of things. A bit sorry, some relaxed, and then, without coming off as an outright monster, as if he would do it all again. Maybe that he would kill whoever you stood in front of him, as long as he thought it was for Ally. In his mind he had taken up a noble cause. A crusade, of sorts. He saw himself as a chivalrous defender of the one who held his heart. It was outrageous, of course. The drugs were the enemy, not the suppliers. Killing the people that had introduced her to them, or kept her stocked, was no better than throwing a cup of water out of the boat, and leaving the hull breached. It would have been a lot though, for a man in his pitiful position, to admit that what he had done to Roker was just plain old jealousy. The way I saw it, despite all his ideas about his good intentions, he was just a jealous hot head that had got a taste for killing people. There had been plenty of men, just like him, through the cells at Stateville, on the way to a turn in their last seat, and I figure half of them probably thought pretty highly of themselves at one time or another.

"Explain how it went with Law." Dave still stood, and looked down on our man. I don't know what he thought about the proceedings, but he was going on with them to the end.

Turner scoffed and said, "It was exactly like you said, at the condo. I did go down and have a couple drinks. As soon as I got back in the door, and saw no one was around, I took that knife, went into his room, and did him there in the bathroom. Can I smoke?"

Dave tilted his head forward only slightly.

"You'll have to tell this again. I would have your word, but I don't think it will be necessary." Dave spoke past him again. "Is it, Mr. Scott?"

Turner's cigarette had nary reached his lips, and now fell from them onto the floor. He turned and looked behind him. The body of the man in the coat had reanimated. He stood, removed his hat, and pulled a knit mask off over his head, revealing the red mustache of Ben Scott. He pressed on his lower back to stretch it, and answered.

"No, DeGrabber. I think that will do fine. The others heard it all too." He gestured toward somewhere beyond the light, and five officers in similar outfits, stepped forward.

Turner looked around. The look on his face was exactly like somebody that had had a shock. For sure not an act. He stood up and turned on the spot, taking it all in. Scott turned to the crate that he'd been banging the hammer on, and slid the top off. He offered a hand down into it, and pulled up Officer Rachel Lynn, of the Chicago Police Department. Not quite a movie star in looks, but a better than average sound alike of Ally Lawrence.

"I shot him." Turner blurted. "Where's Ally?" He nearly screeched the second part.

Dave held the little .32 in his palm, and explained calmly. "We reloaded it with blanks from the props trailer while you were incapacitated. As for your second question; by now, Miss Lawrence is probably back in the condo. You were unconscious for over an hour after John hit you."

Turner shot a disgusted look my way. All I could do was shrug my shoulders at him. It had all been a set up since I'd gone to play pool the night before. While I was out shooting nine ball, Ben had come to the office to tell Dave about Phillip Spencer telling where the real rounds were kept. Dave already had the idea cooked up, and gave it to Ben. Ben had sent men, with the key, to the props trailer, and left only the .32 rounds and Ally's prop pistol, so our frame up idea would play. A call to meet at the Stiletto, that I would stand her up on, to get her out of the way, and a respectable acting job, by officer Lynn on the phone with Turner, was all it took. The most unpredictable thing in the whole show had been my part. I don't mean to sound superior, or anything, but Dave's coverage of my knocking Turner out, had been cursory at best. Luckily our recent employer's import warehouse was not lacking in handy items with which to waylay a man. My weapon of choice, picked on the fly on aisle one, had been a piece of petrified wood that you would have on top of a dresser for holding change and things.

I was Ben's time to shine. He put on his official voice.

"Stand up, Mr. Turner."

Turner got to his feet. I was disappointed that after he had given his noble speech, he let his chin rest on his chest. After acting, for days, like a man that hadn't done anything wrong, he'd lost all sense of showmanship. Ben got the handcuffs on him, and checked that everyone was ready to go, before he gave the command to head back out into the cold. We all made our way together, down the sidewalk, and into the parking area of the next warehouse, where the squad cars had been hid. Dave and I brought up the rear of the procession. It was still bitterly cold, but the sky was clear and the stars were out. I allowed myself a grin, and nudged Dave in the ribs.

"This star's out, Dave."

I know it was a bad joke. Dave just opened his eyes a little wider. Just to let me know he had heard me, and maybe so I wouldn't try it again.

With our murderer in the back of a squad car, we shook hands all around, and made our way back to Dave's sedan. As he motored us back through downtown, taking the scenic route to the office and then to each of our apartments, I thought a little about what we had done. It wasn't a clean way to work, threatening to frame somebody like that. Dave had come up with it on his own. I might have tried to take the job as the new props man for the rest of the filming, and tried to come by some evidence that way, but that's why Dave and I compliment. I wouldn't have been able to sit through all those hours of movies he'd watched. Nor could I have come up with such an unscrupulous method of getting that confession. He would never have got anywhere talking to any of the suspects in the type of venues I had had them in. It had worked though. I thought about asking Dave what the plan would have been if it hadn't worked, but decided that kind of second guessing had no place when success has been had. The whole business had made good time too. I was in bed, and resting easy, by ten o'clock, with the peace of mind that came with knowing I'd soon have the funds to buy a little rug for my floor, and that my feet wouldn't be cold for many more mornings.

16

The next morning, waking up well rested, and even seconds before my alarm sounded, I found the linoleum wasn't quite as cold as it had been. It was a heat wave. A whole thirty-five degrees, by the mercury that hung from a nail outside my little window. I whistled through my morning maintenance and headed down to the corner where my favorite diner sat. Gretta, my favorite waitress in all of Chicago, was working, and served me waffles and hash browns along with my coffee. The morning paper had the events from the night before told as a stroke of brilliance by the Police. They had a picture of Ben, with Turner in cuffs in front of him, that must have been shot early this morning. The detective agency of David and Trait didn't have any mention at all, but that was ok. Ben was good about advertising for us, whenever he was contacted by someone needing less than a murder solved. He was a homicide detective, after all. I took my time with the paper, and the coffee, before I walked the mile and half to the office.

The work wasn't quite done for us with the movie people. When I came through the office door, I found I'd been preceded by Dave, as usual, and Walter Fishman.

"John, would you start on your expense report for Mr. Fishman, please?" Dave said, over the sound of an irate movie director. I told him, sure thing, and got settled in behind my typewriter, while Dave dealt with our client.

The hullabaloo was that Fishman didn't feel like he was our client anymore, since we had sent his leading man up the river. Dave explained to him how that was nonsense, and that he had hired us to, "sort it out". We had done that, and so now, the director or his company, was responsible for all costs and fees for services rendered. Fishman said his movie would have to be canceled entirely. He said there was no way around losing both his male leads, and the negative publicity would sour theatres to showing it. He was being downright nasty about it too. As I typed, my mind went back to when Fishman had told us that he couldn't remember who had suggested the second shot in that scene on the street. Turner remembered it well enough. That made me think Fishman probably had an inkling all along, so I remembered that I had drank doubles, in all my outings. Maybe I had also bought a round for everyone in Williams'.

"My lawyers will have your office, DeGrabber!"

Ahh, two rounds.

After a full hour of listening to Dave defend all his points with the sort of litigiousness that makes lawyers nervous when they hear it from a real human, Fishman gave it up, and told Dave to just mail him the bill and he'd pay it. I pecked away at my typewriter. Fishman could get his own door on the way out, if he wanted to behave that way. He did let himself out too, but caught the tail of his duster in the door. He had to open it back up to free himself, and could only turn his nose up, as he turned away a second time, to try and salvage some dignity.

I asked Dave, after the director had gone from the hallway, "How much should we say that warehouse set us back?"

"The item you used to disable Turner was valued at $150 dollars."

I raised my eyebrows and put another zero on the line.

A while later, we were still there pecking away. I sat back and thought for a moment, then decided to let Dave in on it.

"You know what we never did get an answer to?"

"What's that, John?" Dave didn't look up.

"We never found out who loaded Ally's gun, or exactly what that $500 bucks, that Law had, was from."

Dave leaned back in his chair, and kicked me in the shin as he stretched his legs out under my desk.

"For that, we can only speculate. I only showed

you a part of the things I learned from the troupe's films, you know. Not all of it was so instrumental in our pursuits, but some of it was no less illuminating. You see, Steve Roker and Ally Lawrence were love interests in most of the films. I saw many examples of their performances with others too, but none of them seemed so genuine. I can tell, by the way you say her name, that Miss Lawrence has had an affect on you, even in the short time you've known her. Would you call her, enchanting?"

I was somewhat taken aback, but not so much by the idea, as the word.

"I don't think I would ever say something is enchanting, but I see what you're driving at."

He went on.

"I think that Steve Roker did actually care for her, in a way, and wanted Turner removed just as badly as Turner did him."

I nodded.

"So, you think Roker paid Law to load that gun up, and forget to take it up?"

Dave finished the thought.

"And that way, the next day, Miss Lawrence would shoot Turner. It would have been attributed to a terrible confused accident. This, and now I must admit to reckless speculation, would have had a debilitating effect on her, and would likely have pushed her even closer to Roker."

I gave a low whistle. It upset me to think that those men had tried to lord over Ally like she was some sort of trophy to win. It seemed between Roker and Turner, the poor girl never had a chance at real love. Then, seeing that sort of thinking was probably the kind that Turner and Roker had done, I decided to dismiss the whole thing from my mind.

"Well, I think these Hollywood types should stay in Hollywood. Too much drama for me."

I got my nose back to the typewriter, and started the next line.

* * *

This has been entirely a work of fiction, and all things referenced, either existing or otherwise, are used in a fantastical manner. Be sure to check out the other David and Trait Mysteries. You can find them at www.DavidandTrait.com. Also, please review this book on Amazon. It would be a big help.

CPSIA information can be obtained
at www.ICGtesting.com
Printed in the USA
FSHW012119161219
65173FS